Ghosts Who Went to School

Judith Spearing

Inside drawings by Marvin Glass

AN
APPLE
PAPERBACK

SCHOLASTIC INC.
New York Toronto London Auckland Sydney

Dedicated to Edward A. Spearing

Scholastic Books are available at special discounts for quantity purchases for use as premiums, promotional items, retail sales through specialty market outlets, etc. For details contact: Special Sales Manager, Scholastic Inc., 730 Broadway, New York, NY 10003, (212) 505-3346.

ISBN 0-590-40452-0

12 11 10 9 8 7 6 5 4 3 2 1   10   6 7 8 9/8 0 1/9

Printed in the U.S.A.

28

Contents

NOBODY but a newcomer to Templeton would pass in front of the old Temple House. It had been known as a haunted house for so long that even the oldest people in town had crossed to the other side of the street ever since they could remember. Some people said they didn't believe in ghosts, and tried to explain the lights that shone in the windows at night by saying they were just odd reflections; but nobody could explain why the gate swung back and forth and the shutters creaked when there wasn't the slightest breeze, or why the grass never got overgrown in the summer, as it did in the yards of other empty houses. Nobody knew why these things happened at the Temple House, except of course the Temples — Mr. and Mrs. Temple, and their sons Mortimer and Wilbur — who lived there.

The Christmas Tree
in
the
Park

WILBUR TEMPLE WAS RESTLESS. His brother, Mortimer, was out somewhere, and Wilbur was tired of having nothing to do. He thought about going out and swinging on the gate, but he really wanted something new. He drifted around the house, trying to think of something that would be fun and different, and finally decided he might as well build a snowman in the front yard. He could make it right by the fence, so people going by would wonder how the snowman got there.

He drifted out through the front of the house and down the porch steps to the middle of the yard, where he began rolling an enormous snowball. When it was almost up to his waist, Mortimer came home and said, "Hi, Wilbur. Do you want me to help? I could make the head."

"Where've you been?" Wilbur asked.

"Downtown watching people get ready for Christmas. There are a lot of people shopping, and the store windows look great."

"I sure would like to see the store windows," Wilbur said, wistfully. "I never get to go anywhere."

"I'll ask Mother if I can take you," Mortimer said. "The men from the Men's Club are putting up the lights on Main Street. They left it until kind of late because it's been snowing so much; but they're all out working now, and it's going to look beautiful."

Mortimer came back and said it was all right for them to go downtown if Wilbur would stay with Mortimer. Wilbur's mother was afraid crowds of people would frighten him.

They drifted down to Main Street and around the little square in the center of town. Everywhere they looked, they could see men on ladders, fastening lights to the little trees that had been hung on all the telephone poles. "It'll be beautiful," Wilbur whispered. "I do wish we could have a tree. I'd just love to trim a tree. Say, what are those children doing? And why does that big one look so mad?" He pointed toward the barbershop, and Mortimer laughed.

"That's Mr. Snodgrass' shop, and those are his children. Janie's mad because she has to help paint the window. She was mad this morning, too. Last fall when all the stores had the Halloween window-painting contest, Mr. Snodgrass told his children they could paint the window of the barbershop, but then Willie caught such a cold his mother made him stay in bed. Janie and her girl friend painted the window, and Willie and Barbara didn't get to do any of it. They've been pestering to paint the window ever since, so finally Mr. Snodgrass said they could paint a Christmas scene on it, and Mrs. Snodgrass said Janie had to help them. Janie said she felt dumb painting a picture on the window when nobody else was doing it, but I think it would be fun."

"Maybe we could help," Wilbur suggested. "Or maybe we could paint some other window. I'd like to do something for Christmas this year. We never get to. How come those men in the park are just standing around? Aren't they going to put lights on the big tree? I thought they did every year."

The men who had been trimming the little trees on the telephone poles were all putting their ladders in a pickup truck and asking the men who were standing around the big tree when they were going to start hanging lights on it. Wilbur and Mortimer heard a tall, thin man say, "When we find the long extension ladder, that's when. I don't know what's wrong with the Men's Club lately. We never used to start on these projects until we had all our equipment. No organization, that's what it is. I suppose somebody borrowed the ladder and never brought it back. That's typical. Personally, I'm going over to Charlie's for a cup of coffee before I freeze, and that ladder better be here when I get back or I'm not staying out in the cold any longer."

7

"Oh gosh," a little man with red earmuffs said to the man beside him. "I borrowed the long ladder last fall when I had to fix my roof, and I bet it's still in my garage. I'll go get it, but it'll take me a while to get home and back."

"We might call the electric company. They have that big truck with a ladder they use for changing street lights," one of the men said.

"I don't care who you call, just so we get a ladder," the tall, thin man said. "In the meantime, this meeting is adjourning to Charlie's for half an hour. Let's go."

The men left the boxes of lights by the tree and went away. The people who had been standing around waiting to see the lights go up decided they had better finish their shopping before dark; and in a minute or two the park was deserted, except for Wilbur and Mortimer.

"I bet we could put those lights up, Mortimer," Wilbur said. "See, everything's right here."

"Sure, why not?" Mortimer said. "Then watch what happens when those men come back and find the tree all decorated!" He chuckled. "I'll take the lights up, and you make sure the strings don't get tangled. Gosh, there's an awful lot of them. Do you suppose they should go round and round or up and down?"

"I think straight lines that come together at the top would look good," Wilbur told him. "Then the lights would have a tree shape. Look, here's a big star. That must go right at the top." The star floated

8

to the top of the tree, trailing a string of Christmas bulbs behind it, and Wilbur heard Mortimer mutter, "How on earth do they fasten the things on? Oh, I get it."

A little boy whose mother was hurrying him through the park said, "Listen, Mommy, the tree's talking. I guess it's putting its own lights up because all the men went away. I can see the star at the top."

"Is it, darling?" his mother replied without looking up. "Most anything can happen at Christmas, but let's not stop now. This wind is icy." The little boy walked backward, watching the lights fastening themselves to the tree, until his mother turned

9

him around and said, "Please come on. It's getting late, and we still have to go to the hardware store."

"That's the last string of lights," Mortimer announced a few minutes later. "What's this? Tinsel? Let's hang it around the tree; it'll look pretty."

"This is fun," Wilbur said happily. "Shouldn't those lights be plugged into something, though? There's a plug on the end of this long cord."

"I guess so," Mortimer replied. "It isn't very dark yet, so they won't show much, but we might as well plug them in. There's a socket on this pole. Hand me the cord."

"It's beautiful, just beautiful," Wilbur whispered. "Oh, Mortimer, I wish we could have a tree at home."

Janie and Barbara had noticed the lights on the tree and had come across the street to see who had put them up. When the lights came on by themselves, Janie was about to try to explain to Barbara how it happened when Willie yelled from the barbershop, "You quit that, Hank Bartlett. Give me that brush. Janie, come back here! Hurry! Look what Hank is doing! He's ruined our window."

Wilbur and Mortimer drifted quickly across the street to the barbershop and saw a big boy painting a girl in a bright blue bathing suit at one end of the window. It looked a little odd right beside one of Santa Claus's reindeer. A little boy was jumping up and down in front of him and yelling, "Quit it! Give me that brush." But the big boy just laughed and held the brush out of reach.

"Want to fight me for it, Willie Boy?" he asked,

10

just as Janie and Barbara came skidding along the sidewalk. Barbara began to cry.

"I think this gal would look good on water skis," Hank said, but before he could paint them, something seized his arm and snatched the brush from his hand. A voice said, "Quick, Wilbur, grab him. I want to wipe this paint off before it dries. Hang onto him now." Hank jerked his arm loose, but then his feet went out from under him and he was sitting on a snowbank. It looked as if something was holding him down, but there was nothing there. He struggled to get up, but something on his stomach wouldn't let him move. He began to kick and yell, but still he couldn't get up.

Barbara Snodgrass stopped crying and pointed at a rag that was washing the girl in the bathing suit off the window. The same voice that had told Wilbur to grab Hank said, "Okay, stand him up, but don't let him get away. Since he's so fond of paint, we'll give him some to keep. Here, you, stand up and quit making so much noise." Hank felt himself pulled to his feet, but there was still something holding him tight around the waist. "Are you through with the red, Janie?" the voice asked.

"I — I guess so," Janie said faintly. "I've done Santa Claus and the sleigh and the chimney. I was going to let Willie and Barbie put a tree or something in that corner."

"Good," purred the voice. "I know just what to do with the rest of it." The jar of red paint floated away from the window and upended itself right over Hank. Red paint flowed down over his hair

11

and into the hood of his jacket. Some of it dribbled down his face, too. Hank yelled louder than ever.

Mr. Snodgrass came running out of the barbershop, waving his clippers. A man with his hair half cut ran after him, with the big apron they put on in a barbershop billowing around him. A policeman dashed up the street. The policeman yelled, "Stand back. Let me through. What happened? What's the matter, Mr. Snodgrass?"

"I don't know, Sergeant Markowitz," Mr. Snodgrass replied. "I was cutting the mayor's hair when we heard all this yelling and came out and found Hank here with red paint all over him."

"Those kids of yours," Hank spluttered. "I wasn't doing anything, and all of a sudden they poured paint on me." He was trying to wipe the paint off his face, but the more he wiped, the more he spread it around.

"That's not true," Janie shouted. "He tried to spoil our picture, and then this paint just poured down on him. We never touched it."

"That's right, Dad," Willie said. "He painted a girl in a bathing suit right beside a reindeer, and it looked terrible, and then all of a sudden he just stopped painting and the red paint flew over and poured on him by itself."

"That's right," Barbara said. "And this rag washed the girl off all by itself and the red paint flew . . ."

"I heard," Mr. Snodgrass told them. "I heard, but you don't need to think I believe it."

"You'd better go get cleaned up, Hank," Sergeant

Markowitz said, "and maybe it would be a good idea to leave other people's things alone after this."

"I want to go," Hank said, almost sobbing, "but I can't."

There was silence as a voice asked, "Could I paint a moon and maybe one star right at the top, please?" Nobody answered, so a brush rose to the top of the window and began painting a crescent moon.

The brush finished the moon and painted a little star right at the top of the window. Then it settled into the yellow paint again and the voice said, "Thank you very much. I just love to paint pictures, and I hardly ever get to. Are you still hanging onto Hank, Wilbur? You might as well let him go. We don't want him for anything, do we?"

Wilbur let him go so suddenly that Hank sat down in the snow and started yelling again.

Sergeant Markowitz suddenly remembered Halloween night when he and another policeman had caught two bank robbers at the Temple House. He had never understood just how the robbers had been persuaded to stay and wait for someone to arrest them, but something had kept them there. He was still thinking about that when the voice said, "Just remember, Hank Bartlett, the next time you want to pick on somebody, we might be watching you."

"What . . ." Sergeant Markowitz began, but before he could say anything, a fire engine came roaring down the street and pulled up beside the park. The firemen jumped out and started setting up a

long ladder. Right after it came a bright yellow electric truck with a red light winking on its roof. A man got out and looked at the gate. He called, "Okay, Bill. Right through here and up to the tree. You have plenty of room."

Men from the Men's Club were coming back to the park, and a little white truck that had "White's TV Service" painted on the door was parked right behind the telephone truck. A black station wagon with a long ladder tied on the roof parked right behind it. The little man with the red earmuffs got out and said, "Gosh, if I'd known you fellows would get so many ladders, I wouldn't have gone all the way home for this one."

The tall, thin man who had been so cross yelled, "What's going on? I asked the fire chief if we could use his ladder, but I didn't send for all these trucks."

"My brother-in-law works for the electric company, and I called him," a man in a green jacket explained.

"Say, what kind of gag are you trying to pull, Fred?" the fire chief shouted. "I thought you said you couldn't put the lights on the big tree because you couldn't find a ladder."

"We couldn't," the tall, thin man replied. "I didn't know everybody was going to get a ladder. No organization, that's what it is."

"Just look behind you, will you?" the fire chief said.

Everyone looked around. It was getting quite dark by now, and the Christmas tree lights in the park shone out brightly.

"What . . . who . . . which of you fellows put those lights up without telling anybody?" the tall, thin man asked.

The little boy and his mother came out of the hardware store, and the little boy said, "See, Mommy. Doesn't the tree look pretty? I told you it was decorating itself."

"It's beautiful, darling," his mother replied. "Just beautiful. We'll tell Daddy about it when we get home, won't we? But let's hurry now. I have to get supper, and this wind is freezing."

Nobody but Wilbur and Willie Snodgrass heard Mortimer say, "Come on home, Wilbur. Let's get Mother and Daddy to come see the tree we decorated. I bet it's the prettiest one in Templeton."

Taking
Pictures

THE DAY AFTER CHRISTMAS, Wilbur and Mortimer were thinking about going outdoors when Mrs. Temple exclaimed, "What on earth are those two young men doing?"

Mr. Temple looked out the window and said, "They seem to be setting up a camera on a tripod across the street. It looks as if they're going to take a picture of our house. I wonder why?"

Mortimer looked out and said, "You're right, Dad. But why should they want a picture of our house?"

"Why shouldn't they?" Mrs. Temple asked. "This is a very attractive house. Oh look, the tripod almost fell over. It reminds me of Johnnie Temple. Remember how he was always making people stop what they were doing to have their pictures taken? He had a dreadful time with his tripod, too."

Wilbur laughed and said, "I'd forgotten all about that. Do you remember the time he was taking a picture of Lucy, and Mortimer appeared right behind her? Johnnie worried for weeks about how the boy got into the picture."

"Yes, but why should those men be taking pictures of our house?" Mortimer persisted. "Now they're coming over here."

When Mrs. Temple looked out the window again, she saw that the young men had opened the gate and were setting up the camera in the front yard. "I hope they aren't thinking of buying the house," she said. "I don't like the way that man from the bank keeps bringing people around to look at it. Why don't you go and find out what they're here for, Mortimer?"

Mortimer drifted out through the side of the house to the yard where the young men were taking a picture of the old well. He heard one of them say, "This is perfect, and I don't believe it's ever been written up. Gosh, Tom, with pictures of an old house nobody knows about, if I write any kind of a good paper, it should really bring my grade up. It sure is lucky your sister remembered this place. The only thing is, I'll need pictures of the inside, too. Do you think we could open a window?"

"Sure, Dave, if you want one of the neighbors to call a cop. Sally will just love it if she has to get us out of jail. Didn't you listen to her? She said if we want to go in, we can get the keys at the bank."

"Well, let's get them. I can't write a paper about

17

the house if I don't have some pictures of the rooms. I just hope it's as well preserved inside as it is outside."

While the men had been talking, the one called Dave had been moving around the yard taking pictures, with Mortimer drifting after him. As soon as they left, he went back in and told the family what he had heard. "That tall blond one is writing some kind of paper about houses," he said, "and he wants pictures of the inside of our house. He's going to get the keys from the bank and come back this afternoon. He says the house is perfect, and it's lucky it's so well preserved."

"What does he mean, lucky?" Mr. Temple snorted. "It's hard work, not luck."

"I guess he means lucky for him," Mortimer explained. "You know what would be funny? To put some people in his pictures!"

Mr. Temple laughed. "Of course," he said. "We're well preserved, too. I'll tell you what we'll do. All these photographers spend a long time fussing with their cameras to get everything just right, but it only takes a second to take the picture. While the boy is getting ready, we'll get in the right place, and then we'll appear just for an instant when he takes the picture. If we vanish again right away, he'll never notice us."

That afternoon, the two young men came back to the house with an older man. Mortimer drifted out and heard the older man say, "Yes it is. It's in very good shape, and you'd think it would sell in a minute. People around here like these historical-looking houses, but we haven't been able to sell this one. Of course you'd have to fix it up a lot inside."

"I'm glad it isn't fixed up yet, Mr. Montrose," Dave told him. "My professor wants me to write about something old."

"Even the modern improvements in this one are old," Mr. Montrose said. "A bathroom was put in a long time ago, and there's some primitive wiring, but I don't think there's a woman in the country who'd use the kitchen the way it is. Still, people have bought worse houses than this." He opened the front door and said, "I'll leave the keys here. You can lock up and bring them back to the bank when you're through. Take all the pictures you want."

Dave looked in and said, "I didn't know there'd be furniture."

"Will it be in your way?" Mr. Montrose asked. "I think some of it belonged to the original owners."

"Oh no," Dave replied. "It will look better with furniture."

"Wait till he sees it with people," Mortimer whispered.

Mr. Montrose went back to his car, and the two young men walked through the house, looking at all the rooms. "This is perfect," Dave said. "It ought to get me an A. Let's start with the living room. Come on, help me set up the tripod."

The Temples could see that the first picture was going to be of the corner of the living room with the fireplace, so Mrs. Temple and Wilbur sat down on the couch in the corner. "How will we know when to appear?" Mrs. Temple whispered.

"See that black cord thing?" Mortimer whispered. "This morning when he was taking pictures, he pushed that little button on it to take them. If you appear just when he picks it up, you'll be all right."

"Say, Tom, did you hear a kind of a whispering noise?" Dave asked.

"I expect there are mice in the walls," Tom said. "Do you want this door open or shut?"

"Leave it shut for this picture. I'll take one from a different angle with it open so you can see into the room beyond. Move that candlestick, will you? I want it on the table at the end of the couch so it'll look as if someone has been sitting there reading.

Here, lay one of these books face down on the couch, as if someone has just left it there. Okay — now get out of the way. I don't want a picture of you." As soon as Tom moved away and Dave was looking at the camera instead of the couch, Mrs. Temple picked up the book. The camera clicked, and the light flashed. Wilbur was so surprised he squealed.

"What was that noise?" Dave asked. "Didn't you hear a squeak?"

"Mice," Tom said. "I told you. All these old houses have them."

"They sure are noisy," Dave said. "Help me move the tripod so I can take a picture going into this bedroom. I suppose this was the parents' room and the children slept upstairs. It's a nice-looking room, isn't it? My sister would love that bed. She's crazy about old-fashioned furniture. There. Now let's go out in the kitchen."

In the kitchen, Dave asked Tom to set the table so it would look as if a family were just going to have supper. He found a hook in the fireplace and hung a large kettle from it. "I'll bet the first family that ever lived here used to cook in the kettle over the fire, before that stove was put in," he said. "I'll put this ladle in as if someone were going to serve some stew. Put some bowls on the table, and silver too, for goodness sake. You don't think they ate with their fingers, do you?"

Tom had looked on all the shelves of the big china cupboard without finding any silver. Just as he was about to tell Dave that there wasn't any, Mrs. Temple got impatient and pulled a drawer open so he could see the knives and forks and spoons. "Gosh!" he exclaimed. "That drawer came right open to show me the silver."

"A good thing, too," Dave said. "It's taking you long enough. I've taken three pictures of other parts of the room already."

Tom put the silver beside the plates and went to look for some glasses. Mr. Temple and the boys, who had been sitting at the table, moved the dishes and silverware so the pieces were right in front of them, with another place set for Mrs. Temple, who was standing near the fireplace. When Tom came back with the glasses, he said, "Did I set the table that way? It looks neater, somehow. Is this all right?"

"Fine," Dave told him. "Suppose you sit down with your back to me. The table will look better with somebody at it."

"He's sitting in Mother's chair," Wilbur whispered, but his father told him it didn't matter.

"Now I'm hearing things," Tom said. "This house is creepy, isn't it?" Mrs. Temple had been standing by the kettle, holding the big ladle, for such a long time that when Dave finally snapped the picture, the light from the flash bulb startled her and she dropped the ladle with a clatter. "What was that?" Tom asked nervously.

"Those mice of yours, I guess," Dave said. "No wonder nobody wants to buy the house. One more of the kitchen, and then we'll go upstairs."

On the way up, Dave wanted a picture of the steep, narrow stairway. "I'm glad I don't have to climb these every night to go to bed," he said. "I can hardly set the tripod up here, it's so narrow."

While he was trying to adjust it, Mr. Temple told Mortimer and Wilbur to go halfway up the stairs and appear in their nightshirts, as if they were on their way to bed. Wilbur said he hoped he could remember how to appear in a nightshirt because it was a long time since he'd worn one.

Tom stood by the doorway, watching Dave and

listening to the whispering noises. When Dave took the picture, Tom laughed nervously. "This house is beginning to get me," he muttered. "I almost thought I saw a couple of boys in nightshirts on the stairway for a second. Let's get out of here before I go crazy."

"We can go as soon as I get a few more pictures," Dave said calmly. "I can't go before I get everything I need. And besides, I haven't heard anything lately."

"That's just because you're all wrapped up in that darn camera," Tom insisted, getting more and more jittery.

Dave took a picture of the little room with two narrow beds and a big cupboard in it at the top of the stairs and another one of the attic. Then he said he was done.

"You straighten up the kitchen while I put my stuff in the car, and we'll take the keys back to the bank. I don't want to leave anything out of place when the old fellow was so nice about lending us the keys."

He carried his camera and tripod to the car, and came back to see if Tom needed any help putting things away.

Tom met him at the door. "I must be getting absent-minded," he said. "I thought we left all those dishes on the table, but they were all put away when I went back to the kitchen. Let's go."

When they had gone, Mrs. Temple said, "I wish

we could see the pictures, but I don't suppose we ever will."

About a week later, Wilbur and Mortimer were having a snowball fight in the front yard; but of course all anyone could see was snowballs flying back and forth. Suddenly they saw Tom and Dave drive up, and the boys stopped and waited to see if the two men were going into the house again. Dave got out of the car and said, "Thanks Tom. It's lucky I remembered about getting measurements. I wish I'd thought of it when we were here before. Old Perryman's a bug on dimensions, and if I tried to guess at them, I'd be sure to get something wrong."

"I'll pick you up in about an hour," Tom said. "I'll get the things Sally needs for her class next Monday and I'll see if your pictures are ready, too." He drove off, and Dave unlocked the front door and went in the house.

He started in the living room, measuring walls and doorways with a long tape measure that rolled up in a case when he wasn't using it. He wrote the measurements in a little black book. The Temples followed him all around, but they didn't do anything to disturb him until he was trying to measure the kitchen. For some reason, the end of the tape measure kept wanting to roll up. Just as Dave decided he would have to hold it down with the kettle, the measure lay down of its own accord and inched back to rest against the wall, right where he wanted it. "Thank goodness," Dave said, and wrote the measurement down. "Now the pantry and I'll be done. Let's see, it's . . ."

"Forty inches," a voice whispered.

"Thanks," Dave said, and wrote it down. Then he said, "Huh?" and looked around. He measured the pantry and it was forty inches. "I'm going funny in the head, that's what it is," he told himself.

Just then the front door opened and Tom came in. "I got the pictures," he shouted. "Where are you? Oh, here you are. Let's look at them." He took the pictures from the envelope and laid them on the kitchen table. Both men stared and stared. At last Tom gasped, "Who . . . who . . . who on earth is that? Where did they come from?"

"I like that one of the boys going up to bed, don't you, dear?" Mrs. Temple said.

"It's very good," Mr. Temple replied, "but my favorite is the one of you reading to Wilbur. It's an excellent likeness. I like the one of the kitchen, too."

"I've cooked a lot of meals in that old kettle," Mrs. Temple said. "I guess the stove is better, but I never minded cooking at the fireplace."

"I'm getting out of here," Dave shouted, and ran for the door.

Tom was too surprised to move. He just stood there, staring at the table. At last he saw the pictures gather themselves together and slip into the envelope. Then they came out again, and Mr. Temple said, "Weren't there two pictures of us in the

kitchen? I wonder if he'd mind if we kept one."
Tom didn't answer; he just stood there with his
mouth open. So Mr. Temple laid one picture on the
table and put the others back in the envelope. Tom
still did not move, so Mr. Temple handed him the
envelope. "You'd better take your friend's pictures
to him," he said. "He went off without them."

"He seems to be rather easily frightened," Mrs.
Temple added.

Tom backed away from the envelope and ran
down the hall. When he got to the front door, he
turned and dashed across the porch and down the
steps. Dave was standing on the walk, and he just
stood with his mouth open as Tom came running
toward him with the pictures following after. A
voice kept saying, "Here, take them." Tom ran to
the car and got in the driver's seat.

The yellow envelope full of pictures floated to
Dave and landed in his hand. Something closed his
fingers around it. With that, he jerked himself loose
and ran for the car, but he still had the pictures.
The Temples watched the car start down the street.
It wove from side to side so violently that Mr. Temple said he hoped the boys wouldn't have an ac-
cident.

"Those are very careless young men," Mrs. Temple said. "They didn't even shut the door when they
left."

Wilbur
Goes
to
School

WILBUR AND MORTIMER WERE BORED. When ghosts have been haunting the same house for a long time, and haunting it so effectively that no one goes there any more, there is very little variety for them. For years they hadn't particularly minded staying at home, but after the excitement of catching the bank robbers on Halloween and the fun of decorating the village Christmas tree and appearing in pictures, they found being at home all the time very dull. One morning Wilbur said he almost wished somebody would buy the house so they could have some children to play with.

His father immediately said he certainly didn't want any people moving in, and he was going to go right on making sure nobody would want to buy the house. "It was all right when some of our relatives used to live here," he said, "but I don't intend to have strangers moving into our house. I'd never be comfortable again." Then he said, "I suppose you do need something to do after all these years. Why don't you go to school?"

Wilbur said, "I used to go to school and I didn't like it. I don't want to." But the more his parents thought about it, the more determined they were that Wilbur and Mortimer should go to school.

Mortimer agreed. He said, "You'll like it, Wilbur. Schools are quite different now from what they were when we were alive. You'll meet a lot of people and have a good time." Mortimer often spent half a day or so at school. He wasn't particularly interested in social studies or math, but he liked English fairly well and he loved science. He said, "I'll take you right now. Come on. I think you should go in the third grade. You look about that old. I'll take you to the room, and when the children go to lunch, you wait for me and I'll bring you home. That'll be enough for the first day, and then if you like it you can stay all day tomorrow."

When Mortimer and Wilbur got to school, Mortimer found the third-grade room and said, "Okay, go on in. There's sure to be somebody out sick so there'll be an empty desk where you can sit. Don't forget to wait for me at lunchtime."

Wilbur said, "I'm scared, and anyway the door's shut."

"Well, for goodness sake, nobody can see you. You don't have to do a thing but watch if you don't want to, and you certainly ought to be able to go

29

through a door by this time. Have fun." He gave Wilbur a little push, and Wilbur drifted through the door.

When he got inside the room, Wilbur thought it looked very crowded. The room was full of children sitting at little desks, but there were a couple of empty desks, too. One wall was full of little cupboards that held coats and boots and lunch boxes. Another wall had a blackboard, and along the top of it there was a long strip of paper with the alphabet on it. There were boxes and books and puzzles

on all the shelves, and the long window sill was full too. It held a goldfish in a bowl, a hamster in a cage, and several pots and glasses and jars with things growing in them. The teacher was sitting by the window sill. Wilbur thought she looked very pretty. She had black curly hair and blue eyes. She was wearing a blue skirt and a cherry-colored sweater and high-heeled, cherry-colored shoes.

Wilbur stood by the door a long time and watched the children. They were all writing something on sheets of lined paper. It was the first time Wilbur had been among people when he hadn't had Mortimer there to look after him, and he felt nervous. After a while he realized that nobody was paying any attention to him, so he drifted to one of the empty desks and sat down. There were books inside the desk, and a couple of pencils, and several wadded up sheets of paper.

He was just wondering whether he would dare take one of the books out to read when the teacher said, "Is everybody finished with the letter to Margery? Collect the letters, please, Alan, and put them on my desk. I'm sure Margery will be glad to hear from us, because her mother says she's lonesome and she won't be able to return to school for at least another week." A tall, dark-haired boy took all the papers to the teacher's desk and sat down again.

Then the teacher said, "Now the first reading group may bring books and chairs up here. The rest of you begin page 34 of your arithmetic workbooks. Read the directions carefully and do all ten examples."

Eight children took books out of their desks, picked up their chairs and carried them to the end of the room, where the teacher was sitting by the window. They made a half-circle with their chairs and sat down. All the other children took large red and white paper-covered books out of their desks. Wilbur found one in his desk, too, so he took it out and opened it to page 34.

The girl sitting next to Wilbur raised her hand and asked, "What should we do, Miss Hartley?"

Miss Hartley said, "If you read the directions at the top of page 34, I think you will know what to do, Nina." Then she asked the reading group to open their books.

When Wilbur opened the workbook, he saw that the problems were the kind his father sometimes gave him to figure out, so he found a pencil in the desk and started writing numbers on the lines in the workbook, just as the other children were doing. He dropped his pencil, and as he started to pick it up, one of the boys said, "Oh, Miss Hartley, look."

Miss Hartley said, "Jason, you know we don't interrupt."

Jason said, "But Miss Hartley . . ."

Miss Hartley frowned at him, so he stopped talking; but as soon as she stopped looking at him, he poked the boy sitting next to him and pointed at Wilbur's desk. The boys could see a pencil moving back and forth over the workbook, as if someone were writing in it. After a minute the pencil lay down and the book moved a little on the desk. Then the pencil stood up and began to write again. The boy next to Jason poked the girl on the other side of him and she whispered, "Ouch. Quit it, Bobby." Then she looked where he was pointing and said, "Oh, Miss Hartley, you should see Willie's pencil writing all by itself."

The fat little girl in front of her said, "Maybe the pencil misses Willie and wants to do his work so he won't have so much to make up when he gets well." All the children began to giggle and stare at the desk. The pencil lay down. The book started to slip back into the desk, but Miss Hartley walked over and picked it up. Wilbur felt terribly embarrassed. He hoped Miss Hartley wouldn't put him out. She looked at the book and said, "Somebody must be playing a joke on us. Who's been writing in Willie's workbook? The problem is right, but I think you'd all better do your own work or you won't be finished before lunch."

She went back to the reading group and told the rest of the class to go on with their arithmetic. All the children were watching to see if Willie's pencil would start writing again, but Miss Hartley told them to put their eyes on their own work and watched them until they did. As soon as no one was staring at him, Wilbur started doing some more arithmetic too. He thought it was quite interesting, like a puzzle. When he had finished five problems, Miss Hartley told the second reading group to get their books out. Eight more children got up when the first group brought their chairs back, and Wilbur decided he would like to join them. He was going to take his chair up the way the other children did, but then he thought Miss Hartley might not like to see a chair floating around the room, so he just took his book. He thought if he sat behind the circle of chairs maybe nobody would notice him. He didn't feel so frightened of the class now, but he still didn't want to be conspicuous.

When Miss Hartley told the children to look in the table of contents and find Cinderella, and then turn to the right page, Wilbur found it too. He had often read Cinderella before, but he didn't mind. The first child read very well, and then Miss Hartley asked the next one to read. She read, "The new wife loved her own children, but she was curl . . ."

"Cruel," Wilbur whispered.

"I thought the members of this class knew we didn't help each other until we were asked," Miss Hartley said. "Try it again, Louise. Sound the word out carefully and think. A woman wouldn't be 'curl,' would she?"

"Cruel," Louis said. "She was cruel to her step- — her step- — I can't get that word, Miss Hartley."

"Who can help Louise?" Miss Hartley asked.

Wilbur really didn't want to attract attention, but he couldn't resist showing that he could read. He said, "Stepdaughter."

"Thank you," said Miss Hartley. "Was that you, Alan? It didn't sound quite like you."

"No ma'am, it wasn't me," said the boy in front of Wilbur. "It must have been Bobby."

"It wasn't me," the boy beside Alan said.

Miss Hartley said, "You mean, 'It wasn't I.' That's strange." She looked a little closer. She thought she

34

could see the edge of a reading book floating in the air, sticking out behind Alan's chair. She told herself it must be a trick of the light. She blinked and looked again, but it was still there. She took a deep breath and said, "Marilyn, you may read now." Marilyn read to the end of the page, and all the children turned the page. Miss Hartley didn't really want to look at Alan's chair, but she did and she saw the book in the air turn a page too. She decided she'd better make an appointment to get her eyes examined. It was Alan's turn next, and he read so slowly that he made the story sound like a list of spelling words. Miss Hartley said, "You pronounce the words well, Alan, but try to read a little faster. It's a story. Who will show Alan how it should sound?"

Wilbur knew he shouldn't show off, but the temptation was too much for him. He read, "The stepsisters said Cinderella could not go to the ball with them because they would be ashamed of her rags and ashes."

"Are you trying to be funny, Bobby?" Miss Hartley asked.

"Oh no, Miss Hartley, I didn't read that," Bobby said. "I can't read that well, anyway."

"Who was reading?" Miss Hartley asked. Nobody answered her. Miss Hartley's face got pink and she said, "Tell me right now who was reading."

"I was," Wilbur said.

"Stand up and come here," Miss Hartley said. She saw the book rise up in the air and float toward her. She stood up and backed away, but it came closer. All the children sat with their mouths open. The book stopped in front of Miss Hartley, and a voice said, "I was reading, Miss Hartley."

"I said I didn't do it," Bobby said.

"What is it?" Miss Hartley squeaked. She backed up a little more, right into the goldfish bowl.

"Look out," Wilbur shouted, but he was too late. The goldfish bowl skidded off the edge of the window sill and water splashed into the hamster's cage and all over the floor. Miss Hartley tried to get her balance, but she slipped in the puddle and sat down on the floor. The goldfish flip-flopped in the air, landed on Miss Hartley's lap, and then flopped onto the floor. Everybody was jumping up and down, trying to see better. A little girl at the back of the room shouted, "My hamster! He'll get all wet," and pushed her way through the children and picked up the hamster cage.

Alan said, "My poor goldfish. It'll die!" He tried to pick it up, but he slipped in the water and sat down on Miss Hartley.

Wilbur picked up the goldfish and put it in a glass of water that had a carrot top growing in it. Then he picked up the bowl and took it to the sink to fill it. While he was running water into the bowl, the door opened and a man came in. He saw all the children standing up and yelling and said, "Back to your seats, children. Be still. Miss Hartley, are you all right? Did you fall? What on earth happened in here? I could hear this class all the way down in my office."

The children went back to their seats fairly quietly. Alan got up from Miss Hartley's lap and sat in his chair. Bobby said, "Look, Mr. Graham," and pointed.

Everyone saw the goldfish bowl, three quarters full of water, float away from the sink and set itself gently on the window sill. Then a glass of water with a carrot top in it got up. The carrot came up out of the water, the glass turned itself over, and water and a goldfish poured into the bowl. Then the glass and the carrot top floated over to the sink.

Miss Hartley was still sitting on the floor.

Mr. Graham looked away from the sink and snapped his mouth shut. Then he glared at Miss

Hartley and asked, "Can't you get up, Miss Hartley? What is your class doing today? Are you teaching them to do magic tricks?"

Miss Hartley pulled herself up and whispered, "I don't know what it is." She sat down and wiped her forehead. "This has been a most upsetting morning. You did see it too, didn't you? Oh dear."

The glass, which now had water and the carrot top in it, floated back to the window sill. Then a voice said, "If we had a mop or a cloth, we could wipe up the water before anyone else slips."

"I know where they are," Louise said. "I'll get them." She bounced up and took a mop from the closet, found a rag too, and took them both to the window sill.

"Thank you," said the voice. "You wipe and I'll mop."

All the children watched while Louise held the mop out in front of her. It jumped from her hand and began moving back and forth, vigorously mopping up the puddle. Louise began to wipe the window sill. The mop wrung itself out in the sink and the voice said, "I didn't see where you got this." The mop hung in the air till Louise took it.

A bell rang and Mr. Graham said, "It seems to be lunchtime. You children may line up and go to the cafeteria without your teacher this once. Tell the lunchroom teacher I said it was all right. Line them up, lunch monitor."

All the children were still staring at the window sill, but at last Nina walked to the door and started calling, "People carrying their lunch, those buying milk, those buying milk and dessert, those buying their whole lunch." The children lined up in groups and filed out after Nina. As soon as they got outside the door, they began asking each other who had been in the room.

Mr. Graham said, "You look quite pale, Miss Hartley, and no wonder. I've never seen anything like this and I've been principal five years, and I taught for twenty years before that. Why don't you have lunch with Mr. Humphrey and me in my office? He had rather an odd experience in his science class this morning that he wants to tell me about. Something about moving lights, I think he said. Uh . . . is it . . . well, do you think it's . . . is it still here? Whatever it is?"

Before Miss Hartley could answer, they both heard another voice say, "Here I am, Wilbur. How did you like school?"

Wilbur said, "I was scared at first, but now I like it. It's pretty exciting here. If it's like this every day, I'll come a lot."

"Wait till I tell you what I did in science," Mortimer said. "It's too bad we told Mother and Daddy we'd be home at lunchtime. Never mind, we'll come back tomorrow."

As they drifted down the hall, they heard Miss Hartley say, "If this happens tomorrow, I'm never coming back."

Then Mortimer and Wilbur went home.

Wilbur
and
Mortimer
Appear

Wʜᴇɴ Wɪʟʙᴜʀ ᴀɴᴅ Mᴏʀᴛɪᴍᴇʀ ᴛᴏʟᴅ their parents about school, Mr. Temple said if only people could see them looking like ordinary schoolchildren, they wouldn't cause so much excitement. Mortimer wasn't sure he wanted the excitement to stop, but all he said was, "We'll need some new clothes. If we appear in ours, the teachers will really faint. They're fine for scaring people away from the house, but they don't look like modern school clothes."

"Think some, then," his father said. "You can think modern clothes just the way you do your own, or those nightshirts you wore when that young man was taking your picture."

Wilbur tried to remember what the boys in school had been wearing. He thought Alan was about his size; and he had been wearing a red plaid shirt and blue corduroy slacks. He concentrated very hard, and suddenly appeared in front of his family in a red shirt and blue trousers. "You look awful," Mortimer said. "You can't wear that bright red with your hair, and your shirt's not even tucked in. You ought to think yourself some socks and shoes, too, while you're at it. You can't go to school barefoot." Wilbur stared at his feet, and in a minute or two he was wearing scuffed brown oxfords and faded blue socks. He tucked in his shirt, too. "Well, that's better," Mortimer said, "but for goodness sake try some other color shirt. How about blue?" The red plaid gradually turned to navy blue, and Mortimer said, "That's fine. Now I'll try."

Mortimer concentrated on a maroon plaid shirt and black twill slacks. Just as Wilbur opened his mouth, Mortimer remembered socks to match his shirt and black shoes. Wilbur said, "You look great, Mortimer."

Their mother said, "I like the old style better, but you certainly do look like the boys who walk by across the street. The teachers will never think you're ghosts now."

The next day Mortimer and Wilbur went to school once more. They got there while the children were lining up to go in. They could hear the little children talking about what had happened in the third grade the day before, and the big ones telling each other about the science class. Wilbur still felt bashful about appearing in front of a lot of people, and Mortimer didn't want him to get upset and go home, so they just stood and listened, invisible. Wilbur kept pointing to children and telling Mortimer they were in his class. They saw Willie Snodgrass, the barber's son, and heard Louise telling him how his pencil had started to do his arithmetic for him while he was absent.

Willie said, "I wish my pencil would do it for me when I'm there. Anything could do arithmetic better than I can. If Miss Hartley doesn't stop making me stay in from recess to finish it, I might never come back."

When the bell rang, Louise grabbed a little girl's hand and said, "Go find a partner, Willie," but all

42

the boys wanted somebody else for a partner, and Willie had to go to the end of the line. Wilbur drifted in beside Willie, and Mortimer went with the eighth grade. Since Willie was back today, the only empty desk was right in front of Miss Hartley, so Wilbur sat on the floor beside Willie.

The first thing they did after the opening exercises was check yesterday's arithmetic. When it was Willie's turn, he said, "I was absent yesterday." Louise raised her hand and asked Miss Hartley if Willie shouldn't look in his workbook anyway and see if the pencil had done the problems right.

Miss Hartley sighed and said, "Oh dear. All right, William, tell me what's on page 34 of your arithmetic workbook." Willie told her the first five problems were done and read out the answers. "They're all correct, William," Miss Hartley said. "I still don't see — oh well. See if you can get the other five done during the first reading group. Then if you'll stay in from morning recess I'll show you how to do the next section, since you weren't here when I explained it yesterday afternoon."

"I told you so," Louise said. She jiggled in her chair so her pigtails bobbed up and down. "I told you we had a ghost here yesterday, Willie. It's a lot smarter than you are, isn't it, Miss Hartley? It was in my reading group, too. Do you think he'll come back today, Miss Hartley?"

Nina said, "My mother says there are no such things as ghosts. She says people shouldn't play tricks in class."

"I don't see how it could have been a trick," Bobby began, but Miss Hartley said, "That will do, class. First reading group, please. The rest of you begin your arithmetic on page 35. William, if you'll read the directions at the top of page 34 and look at the examples that are done, I think you'll be able to finish your page."

The first reading group went up and Willie stared at his arithmetic book. He poked at it with his pencil, but he didn't seem to be doing anything. He looked so miserable that Wilbur just had to help him. "Look," he whispered, "take these numbers first."

"Please do your work silently, William," Miss Hartley said.

"I wasn't talking," Willie replied, and looked around to see who was. He poked at the paper some more and drew a picture of a cat in the margin. It was a pretty good cat, but Wilbur wanted him to do his arithmetic. He took the pencil out of Willie's hand and started writing numbers. Willie stared and said, "Hey, look at my pencil!"

Everybody looked around and Miss Hartley said, "Since you can't be quiet, you'd better sit in the hall for a few minutes, William."

Willie said, "But Miss Hartley . . ."

"WILLIAM," said Miss Hartley.

Willie trudged out the door, and Wilbur drifted after him. Willie sat down on the bench and began to cry.

"Please don't cry, Willie," Wilbur said. "I'll help

you with those problems. They aren't really so hard. Honest."

Willie was so surprised he stopped crying. "Where . . . what . . . who are you?" he gasped. He suddenly remembered the time he and his sisters had painted a Christmas picture on the window of his father's barbershop and asked, "Did you ever pour red paint on Hank Bartlett?"

"That was my brother Mortimer," Wilbur said, "but I helped. It was fun."

"But where are you?"

"Right here," Wilbur said. "Look." Willie looked toward the voice. At first he didn't see anything, but then he saw a shadow, and the shadow gradually

turned into a red-haired boy wearing a blue shirt and slacks.

"Gosh!" Willie said. "Gee, I wish I could do that. How do you do it? How come you have bare feet?"

"I forgot the shoes again," Wilbur said, and in a minute he was wearing blue socks and dirty sneakers like Willie's.

"That's wonderful," Willie said. "Can you do it any time?"

"I guess so," Wilbur told him. "I haven't tried very often."

"What's your name? Where do you live?"

"I'm Wilbur Temple and I live in the Temple House on Oak Street."

"The haunted house?" Willie asked. "Are you . . . well, I mean . . . I don't want to be rude but . . ."

"I'm a ghost," Wilbur said. "My whole family are ghosts."

"If I were a ghost, I'd never go to school," Willie said. "Do they make you go?"

"There isn't much to do at home," Wilbur explained. "Now I'm going back to get your workbook and show you how to do those problems. Wait right here."

"Where else would I go?" Willie asked sadly.

Wilbur vanished and drifted through the wall. He picked up the book and Ann said, "Oh look, Miss Hartley, Willie's book wants to go out in the hall with him."

Miss Hartley looked up and saw the book and a

pencil float across the room and bump into the wall. She heard a voice say, "Darn it, I forgot the book wouldn't go through the wall." The door opened, and the book and pencil floated out, but the door didn't shut tight.

Miss Hartley sighed, "Oh dear, not again." After a few minutes she walked over and looked out the door. She saw Willie and a red-haired boy sitting on the bench. She heard Willie say, "It's easy when you show me, Wilbur, but the book makes it so complicated."

The red-haired boy said, "You make it complicated because you try to do everything at once. Just think of one part at a time. Now try this one." Miss Hartley watched while Willie worked a problem. Wilbur watched too, and he said, "Perfect. You did it just right. Now do the next one."

Miss Hartley suddenly felt she had seen the red-haired boy before. She stepped into the hall, and he vanished. "Who was that helping you, William?" she asked.

Willie looked around and said, "That's Wilbur. I guess he's kind of shy. He sure is good at arithmetic, though. Are you still there, Wilbur? Let Miss Hartley see you. Look right over there, Miss Hartley."

Miss Hartley looked, and for an instant she saw the red-haired boy. Then he vanished again. She asked, "Haven't I seen him somewhere?" But before she had time to think of where she might have seen him, there was a loud buzz and the public-address system announced, "Grades One, Two, and Three are invited to the gym to watch the rehearsal for the Junior High School boys' athletic demonstration. Please go quietly through the halls. This will take the place of morning recess."

Wilbur said, "Gosh, what was that?"

Willie laughed and replied, "That's just the PA system. Did you think it was a ghost?"

"I never heard anything like it," Wilbur said.

"Come back in and line up with the rest of the class, William," Miss Hartley said. "Does Wilbur want — oh dear, that's ridiculous."

"You want to go, don't you, Wilbur?" Willie asked. "You can sit beside me."

In the gym, they saw a crowd of boys in white shorts and shirts, standing around talking in the middle of the floor.

As soon as all the primary children were sitting on the benches, the gym teacher told the boys to line up in front of one of the basketball baskets. Each boy was to have three tries to throw a ball into the basket. The older boys were at the front of the line, and most of them put all three of their balls in the basket. Then a short boy wearing glasses walked up to the basket. He looked nervously at the ball and tossed it in the air. Everyone could see that it wasn't going high enough; then it gave a little jump and plopped into the basket. The boy looked surprised and everyone clapped. The gym teacher looked puzzled, but he nodded at the boy to try again. This time the boy threw the ball so high it hit the top of the backboard and sailed away from the basket, but it turned in mid-air and went through the basket again. Everyone gasped and a little girl shouted, "Look at Jimmy!" The gym teacher exclaimed, "How on earth did you do that?"

Jimmy asked, "Should I try again?" and the gym teacher nodded. Jimmy gave the ball a weak little toss, and it went straight in front of him and up through the bottom of the basket and down again. Everybody clapped and cheered when Jimmy's turn was over. After that, the ball throwing went smoothly until the last boy had had his turn. He tossed the ball into the corner, but something caught it, called "Catch, Wilbur," and threw it straight to the empty space beside Willie Snodgrass. Wilbur caught the ball and threw it back. The ball stopped in mid-air and flew back to Wilbur. The gym teacher was racing back and forth, trying to catch the ball, and everyone was standing up, trying to see what made it go back and forth.

Miss Hartley leaned forward and poked Willie. When he looked around, she whispered, "Tell your friend Wilbur to stop it. He's ruining Mr. O'Reilly's rehearsal." Wilbur threw the ball back and called out, "We'd better quit, Mortimer." The ball floated to the corner and lay still.

Mr. O'Reilly and everybody else stared at it for a minute, but it didn't do anything else, so Mr. O'Reilly announced that the next event would be jumping over the horses.

The boys dragged six large leather things to the

middle of the floor and lined up behind them. Each boy ran toward a horse, jumped, grasped the handles, and sailed over. Jimmy was looking so miserable that Wilbur felt sorry for him. "Who's that?" he whispered to Willie.

"Jimmy Falcon," Willie whispered. "Janie knows him. She says he's terrible at any kind of gym, but he's awfully smart. I don't see how anybody can be as bad as he is at an easy thing like gym, but you should see him tie knots. He came to my den meeting once. He can play the drums, too. He and Janie are in the same band class."

It was Jimmy's turn now. He ran toward the horse, but Wilbur could see he wasn't jumping hard enough. He was going to fall on his stomach on the horse, but instead he turned a somersault over the horse and landed on his feet on the mat. The gym teacher said, "Wow! How did you do it, Jimmy? I never saw you go over a horse that way before." Jimmy blushed and walked away without explaining how he did it.

After that there was rope climbing. Most of the boys went at least halfway up and some of them climbed clear to the top, but poor Jimmy couldn't seem to hang onto the rope. Every time he got more than a couple of feet up, he slid down again. He finally gave up and watched the other boys. All of them were coming down when Jimmy, who was hanging onto his rope and looking up at it, shouted, "Look up there!" Everyone looked and saw a tall brown-haired boy clinging to the very top of the rope with one hand and waving the other. He wasn't even wearing a gym suit; he was dressed in a dark red shirt and black trousers. Mr. O'Reilly shouted, "Who's that? You know we never climb the ropes unless we're wearing sneakers. Come down very carefully." The boy immediately vanished and everyone began to yell, "Where is he? What happened? Did he fall?"

Wilbur shouted, "That's Mortimer. Look at him now."

Everybody looked up again and saw the same tall boy, but now he was wearing a regulation white gym suit and sneakers. He was standing on the beam that the ropes were hung from, waving to the children. The gym teacher shouted, "You know you aren't allowed up there. Come right down. No! Stay there. We'll get a ladder and bring you down. Don't move. Don't look down. Hang on."

Everybody else was shouting, too. One of the teachers cried, "He'll fall. I can't bear to look. He'll be killed — I know he will."

The boy smiled at everybody and walked slowly across the beam and back again, way up under the ceiling. Mr. Graham walked out to the middle of the room and held up both hands. The children grew very quiet. Mr. Graham said, "I'm sure if you got up there, you can come down. Come down at once and report to me in my office."

The boy said, "I'll be right down," and he stepped off the beam and vanished. Everybody began screaming again and jumping up and down.

Mr. Graham and Mr. O'Reilly stood by the bottom of the rope with Jimmy, staring at the ceiling. Mortimer nearly bumped into them when he appeared, standing quietly on the floor. He was wearing his shirt and slacks again. Mr. Graham and Mr. O'Reilly jumped backward, and Mortimer bowed to them. They both looked quite pale and frightened. Mr. Graham said, "You can explain this in my office, young man."

Mortimer vanished again and said, "Hi, Wilbur, how did you like the show?"

Wilbur shouted, "You were great, Mortimer. Do some more."

Louise said, "Our ghost's back. Goody!"

Mr. Graham waved his arms around till the room grew quiet. He kept looking at the place where Mortimer had been, but nothing else happened. He told the children to go quietly back to their rooms, and they all lined up and marched out with their teachers.

Miss Hartley told Jason to take her class back. She walked over to Mr. O'Reilly and said, "We both seem to have a problem. I have pencils that write by themselves and books that float in my room."

Mr. O'Reilly wiped his forehead and said, "I feel awful. Did you see that? I'm never going to have a gym demonstration again. What ever happened?"

Mr. Graham said, "You two had better meet me in my office at lunchtime and we'll see what we can do about this. Miss Hartley, I hope you don't mean to tell me that something happened in your room again today?"

Miss Hartley said, "I certainly do. For one thing, something made William Snodgrass get some arithmetic problems right, and I could never do that. I'll tell you all about it at lunchtime."

Jason led Miss Hartley's third grade down the hall, but they didn't really go quietly. Everyone was asking Willie who had been sitting beside him, so he said, "It's my new friend, Wilbur. Will you come every day, Wilbur? School is a lot more fun when you're here. I might even get my arithmetic done so I could go out for recess."

"I hope I can come again," Wilbur said, "but Miss Hartley seemed kind of mad. She might not let me."

"How could she stop you?" Willie asked.

"If I'll be your partner in line, will you introduce me, Willie?" Jason asked.

"No, be my partner," Alan and Bobby begged.

"I'm going to be Wilbur's partner," Willie told them.

Willie
Goes
Visiting

FOR SEVERAL DAYS AFTER THE REHEARSAL for the athletic demonstration, nothing unusual happened in school. Mr. O'Reilly began to talk about having the demonstration after all. Miss Hartley stopped watching empty desks as if she expected books to jump out and bite her. Willie Snodgrass became so irritable that his mother said she was going to take him to the doctor, and he got zero in arithmetic twice in a row.

Once Miss Hartley said she almost wished the ghost would come back if that would improve Willie's arithmetic or his disposition. Everybody else was too busy planning Valentine parties to think about anything to do with ghosts.

Every morning on his way to school, Willie left a little early so he could walk past the Temple House, but he never saw anything but the house itself, sitting in the middle of a snow-covered yard. In the afternoon he walked by it again. His mother couldn't understand why he was late getting home every day, but he was so cross when he did get home that she stopped asking him.

The day before St. Valentine's Day, Willie walked past the Temple House again, on his way home from school. He walked very slowly, and when he came to the gate he started to open it. Then he stopped and just stood there with one hand on the latch, kicking at the snow. He looked at the house for a long time. Once or twice he unlatched the gate, but then he shut it again. A tear rolled down his face, and he wiped it away with his mitten. He sniffed, and was turning away when he heard a voice call, "Willie, wait a minute."

Willie turned back and waited. "Willie," the voice said, "please come in. I'm not allowed out, but you could come in. Mother said so. Just open the gate and come in, please Willie." Willie unlatched the gate and opened it. He looked at the house again and walked a little way up the sidewalk toward it. The gate swung shut and latched behind him. "Oh, Willie, I'm so glad to see you. I saw you go by every day, but Mother wouldn't let me go out. Aren't you glad to see me, Willie?"

"I *can't* see you," Willie said crossly. "Why didn't you ever come to school again? I thought we could have so much fun, and then you never came. I got zero in arithmetic twice."

"Oh, Willie, here I am. Right here." Wilbur said, laughing. "Look."

Willie saw Wilbur standing in front of him and asked, "Where's your coat? You'll freeze."

Wilbur said, "That's why you couldn't see me before. I don't get cold when I'm invisible, and I was so excited I couldn't think clothes and talk to you at the same time. Wait a minute." Willie saw a jacket exactly like his own appear on Wilbur. Then he saw a woolen hat, with a little tear in the brim like his, and a pair of black boots.

"Hey, your clothes are just like mine!" Willie said. "That's neat. How do you do it?"

"I just can," Wilbur told him, "but I have to concentrate."

"Oh, Wilbur, aren't you ever coming to school again? We could have such a good time. That was neat in the gym."

"That's why I couldn't go back," Wilbur told him. "My mother heard about it somehow, and she knew right away it was Mortimer and me. Dad thought it was funny, but Mother said we were just showing off, and that's why she kept us home. I don't know if I can ever go again."

Just then a car stopped in front of the house and two men got out. Wilbur whispered, "O-oh, I know that old one. He works at the bank, and lately he's always trying to get people to buy our house. Don't go away, Willie, even if I disappear. Promise? Let's listen to them and see what they want. Okay?"

The younger man said, "Look, Mr. Montrose, where did those boys come from? I thought you said nobody came near this place because they think it's haunted."

"That's funny, I never saw anyone here before. That's the only good thing about this ghost story. There's been no vandalism, even though the house has been empty so long. It's in wonderful shape for such an old place, and there's no reason why we shouldn't be able to get rid of it. We're counting on your agency to sell it for us. If that doesn't work, we may have to give it to the village for a historical museum. Then we wouldn't have to pay the taxes on it; but we wouldn't get back the money that we've already sunk in it. I'll show you around."

The two men walked up to the porch, and Mr.

Montrose said, "Be off, boys. You have no business here; this is private property." Wilbur vanished, and Mr. Montrose gasped, "Where did he go?"

Wilbur said, "I'm right here. I live here, and my friend Willie is visiting me. You can't send us away."

"Don't be funny, boy," the younger man said. "Just run along like your friend. Scoot."

"Don't you dare scoot, Willie," Wilbur said. "Let's go in and I'll introduce you to Mother and Daddy." The front door opened, and the two men saw Willie walk inside. Then the door slammed shut in their faces.

The young man said, "You don't suppose this place really is haunted, do you?"

"Don't be ridiculous, Jackson," Mr. Montrose snapped. "That boy broke in somehow and unlocked the door. Come on in."

He tried to turn the doorknob, but the door was locked. He took his key out and said, "I hope there aren't any more of them in there." He unlocked the door and opened it.

The two men could see Willie standing by himself in the empty room. The sun streamed in the windows, so they could see that the windows were quite clean and there was no dust anywhere. They heard a boy's voice say, "This is Willie Snodgrass, Mother and Daddy. Willie, these are my parents, and you've seen Mortimer before."

Willie whispered, "How do you do?"

Then a man's voice said, "How do you do, Willie? It's a long time since anyone visited us, but we're glad to see you."

Mr. Jackson clutched Mr. Montrose's arm and said, "What is this?" His voice squeaked, and he looked pale.

"Boy must be a ventriloquist," Mr. Montrose said. "Here you, boy, didn't I tell you this is private property? If you'll run along right now this minute, we won't call the police."

"Certainly you won't call the police," the man's voice said. "This is my house. If my son chooses to bring a guest home, it's hardly your affair. In fact, I suggest that you take your own advice and run along."

Mr. Jackson started to back toward the door, but Mr. Montrose stayed where he was. "Boy," he said sternly, "I don't know how you do it, but we've had enough. Out. Go. Understand?"

Willie began to look a little frightened, and a woman's voice said, "Don't worry, Willie. I'm sorry these men had to come just as you got here, but we'll soon get rid of them, and then you and Wilbur can play. Would you feel better if you could see us?"

"I th-think so," Willie quavered.

"Of course he would," Wilbur said. "He's not used to ghosts. I think he was very brave to come in."

Wilbur appeared, still wearing the jacket and boots like Willie's. Then Willie and the two men saw a tall man dressed in very old-fashioned clothes and a woman in a long, full-skirted lavender dress with a white ruffle around the neck. Her auburn hair was pulled smoothly back from her face and wound in a big knot on the back of her head. Wilbur was holding Willie's hand and he asked, "Do you feel better now, Willie?"

"Your mother's beautiful," Willie whispered. "Where's Mortimer?"

"Here I am," said another voice, and Willie saw the tall boy who had been in the gym.

Mr. Jackson was trying to open the door, but since he was pushing instead of pulling, the door stayed shut. Even Mr. Montrose looked a little surprised.

Wilbur's mother said, "My, it's cold in here. I wonder if we should light a fire in the furnace. If you're going to have your friends over often, Wilbur, I think we'll have to make the house more comfortable."

"I haven't lit a fire in that furnace for years," Mr. Temple said. "I don't know if it still works, but we could try."

Mr. Montrose's mouth opened and shut, but he didn't say anything.

"We could at least go into the parlor and sit down." Wilbur's mother led the way into a big room that had several old-fashioned-looking chairs and a sofa with a curved back. There was also a big mirror with a gold frame. Mrs. Temple sat down on the big couch and spread her skirt out.

Willie whispered, "Your mother's skirt looks pretty spread out like that."

Wilbur said, "Come sit over here with me, Willie," and the two boys sat down in a very large chair.

Mr. Montrose had followed them into the room, and Mr. Jackson stood in the doorway, looking in. Wilbur's mother said, "Will you excuse us if we disappear, Willie? It's awfully cold. We'll be right here, you know." All the Temples but Wilbur vanished. He said, "I'll keep my coat on."

Mr. Jackson cleared his throat once or twice and at last said, "I don't believe my agency will be able to sell this house, Mr. Montrose. I think I'll run along now."

"Certainly you won't be able to sell this house," Mr. Temple said. "How can you sell something that doesn't belong to you?"

"This house belongs to the bank," Mr. Montrose said. "We pay the taxes on it and we're going to sell it through this young man's agency."

"I don't think so," Mr. Jackson said.

"Don't be ridiculous," Mr. Temple said. "Why, I've lived in this house for a hundred years. You don't think I'm moving out of my own house just because you tell me to, do you? I built this house, and I've lived here ever since. It's my house and here I stay."

"Don't be silly," Mr. Montrose said. "I don't know what your claim is, but I do know that Mrs. Mary Temple got a mortgage on this house from our bank in 1921. She died before it was paid and nobody else in the family paid it, so we own the house. I don't know who you are, but you certainly have no right to be here."

"My name is Mortimer Temple, and my father was one of the first settlers in Templeton," Mr. Temple said angrily. "I have every right to be here."

Willie looked from Mr. Montrose to the space

where Mr. Temple was. "I've got an idea," he said.

"Nonsense," Mr. Montrose said. "Mind your own business, boy. I'll call the police. They'll make short work of all of you."

"I hope he calls the one who came for that bank robber," Mortimer said.

"The police won't see us unless we want them to," Mr. Temple said. "You'll feel pretty silly when the people at the bank hear you've been seeing ghosts, won't you?"

"We'll have the place torn down," Mr. Montrose shouted.

"You will not," Mr. Temple replied.

"I have an idea," Willie said.

"Don't keep interrupting, boy. Just go."

"Stop telling my guest to go," Mr. Temple roared.

Mr. Jackson said, "I'll wait for you in the car, Mr. Montrose, but I'll tell you right now we'll never sell this house, and I doubt if you can get anyone to come close enough to tear it down."

"You'll stay right here unless you want it all over town that you were scared off by a ghost. That'll make a nice story, won't it? You said your agency could sell anything, and I'll hold you to it."

"Not this place," Mr. Jackson said, but he came back to the parlor.

Mr. Montrose said, "We've got to sell it. The bank doesn't want the place. Never did, in fact. Got stuck."

"Take the men some chairs, Mortimer," Mrs. Temple suggested. "Maybe if they're comfortable, they'll be more reasonable."

A chair slid across the floor to Mr. Montrose, and he felt himself pushed firmly into it. Another chair moved toward Mr. Jackson, but he kept backing away until he was in the corner.

"Chair got you cornered, eh?" Mr. Montrose sneered. "Sit down, nincompoop. I still think it's a trick of this boy's." He glared at Willie.

"If you'd come to me in a friendly way and talk things over, we might come to some agreement," Mr. Temple said, "but I will not be bullied in my own house."

"And I won't talk business with a figment of the imagination."

"So I'm a figment, am I?" Wilbur's father

64

shouted. "If you weren't so old, I'd show you who's a figment."

"I have an idea," Willie said.

"For heaven's sake, tell us the idea then, if you have to," Mr. Montrose snapped.

"Why can't the bank give the house to the village for a museum, the way you said? Then you could stop paying taxes, and the Temples can live here and be the caretakers of the museum."

"A caretaker in my own house?" Mr. Temple asked. "Don't be silly."

"They could show people around and tell them all about Templeton in the old days, and about the furniture and everything. They'd look great. On our vacation last year we went to Williamsburg, there were all these people in costumes to show you through the houses. It was neat. Mrs. Temple could show people how they cooked in the old days, and maybe spinning or making candles or something, and school classes would come, and it would be a lot of fun. And the Temples could just go on living right here. Maybe you could put in a new furnace, too. It sure is cold in here."

"Don't be silly," Mr. Temple and Mr. Montrose said. Then they both said, "Well . . ."

"I never made a candle in my life," Mrs. Temple said. "I do know how to spin, though. It might be fun."

"I'll think it over," Mr. Montrose said. "I'll be back. Don't think I won't. Come on, young man, do you want to stay here all day? I don't." He rushed out with Mr. Jackson after him.

65

"Good," Wilbur's mother said. "They've gone. Willie, I'm sorry we've had all this fuss on your first visit. I hope your next one will be pleasanter."

"I'd better go too," Willie said. "My mother will skin me if I don't get home soon. But please, Mrs. Temple, won't you let Wilbur come to school again? Tomorrow's our Valentine party. He'd like that, and I'd like him to be at school. We could have so much fun together."

"I think you should let him go," Mr. Temple said. "The boys really do need something to do."

"I got zero in arithmetic twice," Willie told them, "and Miss Hartley said she wished something would happen to bring my grade up again. I think she meant she wished Wilbur would come back."

"All right," Mrs. Temple agreed. "Wilbur and Mortimer may go to school, but if I hear of any more shenanigans, they'll stay home forever."

"Oh, thank you, Mrs. Temple. You'll have a good time at the party, Wilbur. I'll see you in school to-morrow. I better run now. Good-bye."

St. Valentine's Day

On St. Valentine's Day, when Willie was getting ready for school, he acted so cheerful that Mrs. Snodgrass hoped whatever had been making him cross was over for good. Instead of glaring at his family and poking his food around, he beamed at everyone and ate his oatmeal without even asking why they never had anything good for breakfast. He gave everyone a valentine and told Janie it was too bad she was in junior high and too old to have a party at school. Then he grabbed his books and paper bag full of valentines and ran out the door.

He decided to walk down Oak Street and see if he could meet Wilbur and walk to school with him. When he got to the Temples' house, he heard Wilbur call out, "Good-bye, Mother, we'll be good; won't we, Mortimer?" Willie saw the front door swing shut. Then a paper bag floated along the walk toward the gate. When it got to the gate, the bag bumped into it and bounced back. Wilbur's voice said, "Ow," and the bag swung over the gate.

"Someday you'll pull your arm out doing that," Mortimer's voice said. "If you could remember to open the door for the bag, why did you forget the gate?"

"I guess I'm excited," Wilbur said. "Hi, Willie, here we are. Mother said you might stop for me this morning. Look, I even have valentines for the party. Mother helped me make them, and she gave me this one for Miss Hartley. Someone gave it to her when she was teaching school before she married Daddy. Isn't it pretty?" The bag opened in front of Willie, and a large cardboard valentine popped out. It had a fat pink heart edged with real lace and surrounded by tiny pictures of birds and flowers. A ribbon across the middle of the heart said, "To my dear teacher." Wilbur had pasted a strip of pink paper across the bottom and had written, "From Wilbur Temple," on it. "I had to cover up the name that used to be there," he explained.

"Gosh, that's beautiful," Willie said. "I bet it'll be the prettiest one in the whole room. Miss Hartley will love it. Come on, we don't want to be late."

When they were about a block from school, Mortimer said, "I don't know if you've noticed it, Wilbur, but people are staring at that bag of yours. Why don't you either appear or let Willie take it for you? We don't want to start a riot before we even get to school."

TO MY DEAR TEACHER

FROM WILBUR TEMPLE

"Maybe Willie'd better take it," Wilbur said. "Here, Willie." The bag jumped into Willie's hand and Mortimer said, "You shouldn't be so bashful, Wilbur. No one will notice you if you appear. You look just like anyone."

"Later, maybe," Wilbur said. "But you can appear if you want to."

"Oh well, not right now, I guess," Mortimer replied.

As they got closer to school, they kept meeting more children. Willie said, "There's Alan and Jason. There's Nina, too. Hi, everybody."

"Who were you talking to?" Jason asked. "How come you've got so much stuff today, Willie? You didn't carry your lunch, did you? It's supposed to be spaghetti this noon."

"Maybe he's talking to that ghost he says he knows," Alan said, laughing. "Whatever happened to Wilbur, Willie? I thought you said he liked school. If he likes it so much, why doesn't he come back?"

"I told my mother we had a ghost, and she said there's no such thing as a ghost," Nina told them. "She said if Miss Hartley lets children play jokes on her like that she can't be a very good teacher and Mr. Graham should speak to her. She thinks it's a trick of Willie's."

"How could I be a trick of Willie's?" Wilbur protested. "He wasn't even there the first day I came."

"Quit it, Willie," Nina said, but she backed away until Alan and Jason were between her and Willie.

"You have quite a load there, Nina," Mortimer said. "Wouldn't you like me to help you carry it?" He took Nina's books from under her arm, and she saw them float down the sidewalk ahead of her.

"Ooo," she squealed. "What is it? My books! Willie Snodgrass, you stop that or I'll tell."

"What did I do?" Willie asked innocently, but he couldn't help laughing.

"Don't tease her, Mortimer," Wilbur begged. "Don't forget what Mother said."

"Okay, here's your stuff," Mortimer said, and the books floated back to Nina. "Take them, stupid. Do you want me to drop them in the snow?"

Nina just stood there until Jason grabbed her books and said, "Come on, Nina. Do you want to make us late?"

"But my mother said there aren't any ghosts," Nina said tearfully.

"Don't start crying now, for goodness sake. Just come on. There's the first bell. Run." Jason ran so fast he dropped Nina's notebook, but Wilbur grabbed it before it fell, so the children who were lining up to go in saw Nina running toward them with her notebook flying after her. When she came to the end of the line, the notebook floated into her hand, and Wilbur said, "Here. Hang on to it."

"Hey, Nina, have *you* got a ghost now?" Louise asked.

Nina just sniffed, but Jason whispered, "Be quiet, can't you? Do you want to get Miss Hartley in trouble? Just march in and keep your mouth shut for once, if you know how."

As soon as they were in their room, all the children went from desk to desk, dropping valentines into the valentine mailboxes they had made the day before. "It's too bad you weren't here to make a mailbox," Willie whispered to Wilbur, "I'm afraid you won't get many valentines because nobody knew you were coming back, but I have one for you, anyway. Hey, watch what you're doing — that's got Jimmy's name on it, and this is Jason's box."

Wilbur jerked the valentine back just in time and said, "I guess I can't read my own writing. Here's Jason's."

71

Everybody was so busy that only Miss Hartley noticed that Willie was carrying two bags instead of one, like everybody else. She wondered why, and she noticed that while Willie was getting a valentine out of one bag, another valentine came out of the other one and dropped into a box by itself. She shut her eyes a minute, but when she opened them, Willie's second bag was still releasing valentines by itself.

Miss Hartley reminded herself that she had said she would even be willing to have a ghost in her class if only William would cheer up. He certainly seemed more cheerful this morning, and he seemed to be talking quite a lot, even though she couldn't see whom he was talking to. She decided to keep a safe distance from the goldfish bowl and see what happened.

When all the valentines were delivered, the children put their bags in their desks and sat down. Willie was the last one to go to his desk because he stopped by Kathy's desk and tucked one of his bags inside it. Then he leaned over and seemed to be whispering to someone in the chair, but of course the chair was empty, because Kathy was home with the measles. Miss Hartley shut her eyes again, and when she opened them, there was still no one at Kathy's desk and William was sitting quietly in his own chair.

After the opening exercises, Miss Hartley told the class to take out paper and pencils for the spelling test. When somebody groaned, she said, "We have to do some work, even on party day. I hope you've all studied your words." She couldn't help looking at Kathy's desk, and when she did, she saw a piece of paper on it, with a pencil poised above the paper ready to write. "Don't forget to write your names at the top," she said, and saw the pencil write something at the top of the sheet of paper. Willie was watching too, and Miss Hartley thought he looked quite pleased.

Miss Hartley picked up her spelling book and said, "Ready? I'll say the word, use it in a sentence, and say it again. 'February. February is a cold month. February.'" She read twelve words and then told the children at the end of each row to collect the papers and bring them to her desk. Meanwhile everyone else was to get out arithmetic workbooks and turn to page 46. Jason was collecting the papers from Kathy's row, and he almost passed right by her desk. Then he saw the paper lying on it and raised his hand.

"Yes, Jason?" Miss Hartley said.

"Do you want this one too, Miss Hartley?" he asked. "It looks like a spelling paper."

Miss Hartley glanced at Willie and saw that he was staring at Kathy's desk and seemed to be trying to say something silently. Miss Hartley was about to answer Jason when the paper rose from the desk and added itself to the pile in Jason's hand. "I think you might as well bring it, Jason," she said. "It seems to want to come up and be read." She looked back at Willie, and he was smiling and nodding as

if she — or else the paper — had done just what he wanted.

Jason winked at Willie. Then he looked at the paper and said, "The spelling doesn't look very good."

"I'll correct the spelling, Jason," Miss Hartley said. "You bring the papers to me and start your arithmetic."

"I bet our ghost is back," Louise said. "Remember the day Willie was absent and . . ."

"Louise," Miss Hartley said, "you must learn to raise your hand before you speak. Now start your arithmetic."

Louise opened her book, but she kept staring at Kathy's desk. In a minute she said, "Look, Miss

Hartley, there's an arithmetic book on Kathy's desk, and it wasn't there a minute ago."

"Would you like to do your arithmetic in the hall, Louise?" Miss Hartley snapped. "At least no one is talking at Kathy's desk, and no one should be talking at yours." Miss Hartley hardly ever got cross, and the children were so surprised that they all started their arithmetic right away.

Miss Hartley forced herself to begin with the top paper in the pile, but she checked the first few papers so quickly that she didn't even notice that Margery had forgotten to use a capital *F* for "February" and Bobby had left the *e* out of "heart." When she came to a paper in an unfamiliar writing, she took a deep breath and looked around. At Kathy's desk, the pencil was busily writing in the arithmetic workbook and the rest of the class was watching it, but Miss Hartley glared so fiercely that the children went back to their arithmetic. The name at the top of the paper was Wilbur Temple, and Miss Hartley remembered that the red-haired boy she had seen for an instant in the hall was named Wilbur. The writing was fairly neat and rather old-fashioned, but the spelling was atrocious. Out of twelve words, eight were wrong. Miss Hartley wrote the correct spelling in red beside each wrong word and at the bottom of the paper she wrote, "Study these words," in large red letters. She told herself that a person who couldn't spell any better than that certainly belonged in school, whether she could see him or not. Miss Hartley thought good spelling was very important, and she made up her mind right then that she would have to keep Wilbur in her class.

When she had corrected the rest of the papers, she asked the class if they had finished their arithmetic. Nobody answered. The children had been so busy watching Kathy's desk that they hadn't done more than two or three examples.

"All right," Miss Hartley said, "I think we'd better do some at the board. I'll read the example and you write down the numbers. When I say 'what,' draw a line and then write the answer on top of the line. Bobby, Margery, Ann, and William go to the board please, and don't look at each other's work." As soon as she called William's name, she thought she should have sent someone else, but it was too late now.

"Ready? 7 plus 3 equals 5 plus what?" Ann, Bobby, and Margery wrote 5 in the blank. Willie wrote 10.

One of the children raised his hand and said, "William's answer is wrong, Miss Hartley," and just then the eraser flew up and wiped out the 10. Then a piece of chalk jumped up and wrote a neat 5 in its place.

Everyone gasped, and Bobby asked, "How did you do that, Willie?"

Louise said, "I . . ." but Miss Hartley said, "Louise, you didn't raise your hand. 10 minus 6 equals 2 plus what?"

This time Willie wrote the numbers down and

stared helplessly. Everybody was watching, and the room was so quiet that the whole class heard a voice whisper, "Think, Willie. What's 10 minus 6?"

"4," Willie whispered back.

"Okay. Now what do you have to add to 2 to get 4?" Willie looked blank and the voice whispered urgently, "Oh Willie, what's 4 minus 2?"

"2?" Willie asked hopefully.

"Well of course. Write it down." Willie wrote it down, but he said, "I still don't get it."

"Never mind. I'll explain it later," the voice whispered.

Margery edged away from Willie and looked nervously at Miss Hartley. Louise noticed her and said, "Don't be afraid, Marge. It's just our ghost that I was telling you about. You were absent when he was here before. That was a lot of fun. Do you . . ."

Just then the bell rang for recess. Miss Hartley said, "You may put on your coats and go out, but I'd like William to stay here a few minutes." The class scrambled into their coats and hats and boots, talking all the while about Willie's arithmetic. Miss Hartley said, "Ann, you're leader this week. Please tell Miss MacIntosh I can't come out. We'll open our valentines when you come in."

As soon as the class had filed out, Miss Hartley asked Willie if he had a guest with him. Willie nodded and whispered, "Yes, Miss Hartley."

"It's all right, I won't eat you," Miss Hartley told him. "Is he still in the room, or did he go with the rest of the class?"

77

"I don't know," Willie replied.

"Well, he's the worst speller I ever saw," Miss Hartley said. "He's as bad at spelling as you are at arithmetic. I think you could help each other a lot if he wants to come to school, but he's got to stop distracting everybody or we'll never get any work done. Find out if he's still here and bring him up to the desk where I can see him, please."

Willie asked, "Are you still here, Wilbur?"

"Sure," Wilbur said.

"Come up to the desk where Miss Hartley can see you," Willie said. Nothing happened.

"Isn't he coming?" Miss Hartley asked.

"I'm right here," said a little voice beside Willie.

"Appear for Miss Hartley," Willie said.

"Later," the voice whispered.

"Now," Willie said firmly. "Miss Hartley can't talk to you if she can't see you. She isn't used to ghosts the way I am."

"I can't," the voice said.

If there was one thing Miss Hartley understood, it was bashful children. She felt quite different about Wilbur when she heard how nervous he sounded. She said, "I want a glass of water. I'll be right back," and walked out of the room without looking behind her.

When she returned, she saw Willie and the red-haired boy standing by her desk. She heard Willie say, "It's different if Miss Hartley tells you to appear. Your mother said not to cause trouble, and it always causes trouble if you don't do what the teacher says. Just let her see you and you can probably come every day and we'll have a good time."

Miss Hartley sat down at her desk and asked, "Is this Wilbur?"

The red-haired boy started to dissolve, but then he came back and Willie said, "This is Wilbur Temple, Miss Hartley. He wants to come to school because he likes it, but his mother found out about what happened in the gym and made him and Mortimer promise not to cause any more disturbance."

Miss Hartley smiled at the boys and said, "Now I know where I've seen you, Wilbur. It was in a picture. Did two boys take pictures of your house at Christmastime?"

Wilbur nodded and said, "Yes, Miss Hartley."

"One of them is my brother Tom," Miss Hartley said. "He and Dave wondered and wondered how people got in those pictures. Your family gave them a good scare. You talked to them, too, didn't you? Dave decided he'd have to use the pictures anyway, because he didn't have time to get any others, and his professor was delighted with them. He gave him an *A* and told him he deserved a lot of credit for going to the trouble of getting people to dress up in the right kind of costumes. Now he wants Dave to send them to some magazine that's having a contest. You know, I'd like to have you come to school, Wilbur, but I don't think Mr. Graham would like it if he knew that one of my students was always disappearing."

"I can't help it," Wilbur said. "I can't explain very well, but it's hard for me to be so you can see me. I have to concentrate on it, and then I can't think about my work very well."

"Oh dear," Miss Hartley said. "That is a problem. Do you think if you practiced, you'd get better at appearing?"

"Maybe," Wilbur said doubtfully.

"Do you suppose you could appear part of the time — say at roll call and when you're reading aloud or answering questions — and then if you just have to, you could vanish when you're studying or writing something?"

"Maybe," Wilbur said again.

"Sure you can," Willie said, "I'll remind you. It'll

be fun if you're here. He brought you a valentine, Miss Hartley. Get it, Wilbur."

"I put it on the desk this morning when Miss Hartley wasn't looking," Wilbur said.

Miss Hartley looked through the pile of valentines on her desk until she found Wilbur's. "Its beautiful!" she exclaimed. "Why, it's the prettiest valentine I've ever received. Thank you very much, Wilbur. William, the class will be back in a minute and I want you to introduce Wilbur and explain that he'll be here every day, even if we can't see him all the time, and we'll treat him just like any other member of the class. Wilbur, I want you to appear while you're being introduced. Will you, please?"

"I'll try," Wilbur said.

When the class had settled down after recess, Miss Hartley said, "I opened a valentine while you were out and I'd like to show it to you." She held up Wilbur's valentine so everyone could see it. "Isn't it pretty? It's from a new member of our class who's a special friend of William's. William will introduce him now. Will you come here please, William, and bring Wilbur?"

Willie walked to the front of the room and said, "Come on, Wilbur." Nothing happened, so Willie went on very quickly, "Our new boy is Wilbur Temple, and he's a ghost. He can appear sometimes, but he's kind of bashful. Do you remember the boy in the gym last week? That was Wilbur's brother. Wilbur's going to come every day and do regular schoolwork, but we'll have to do our work too and not stare at him all the time. You'll like him. He brought valentines for all of us, too."

He started to walk back to his desk, but Miss Hartley said, "Wait a minute, William. I want the class to see Wilbur. Please, Wilbur, just for a minute, anyway."

Everybody stared, and in a minute they saw a shadowy form, which gradually turned into a red-haired boy who was smiling shyly. Everybody laughed and clapped. Louise said, "Where are his shoes?" Wilbur vanished, and Miss Hartley said, "LOUISE."

Wilbur reappeared wearing shoes and socks, and everybody clapped again. Alan said, "Boy, I wish I could do that. Could you teach us how?"

Miss Hartley said, "Even if he could, I don't think I could stand a whole class that kept disappearing. Thank you, Wilbur. We're very glad to have you with us."

"Does Mr. Graham know about Wilbur?" Louise asked.

"Raise your hand," Miss Hartley said. "I don't think we need to bother Mr. Graham right now. Let's open our valentines before lunch."

Ghosts
in
the
Garden

Early one evening in April, Wilbur and Mortimer were resting on their front steps, watching a policeman returning to his patrol car.

"Look who's coming now," Wilbur said. Mr. Montrose and a much younger man were walking down Oak Street. They met the policeman at the gate.

"Good evening, Sergeant Markowitz," Mr. Montrose said. "I hope there's no trouble here."

"Good evening, Mr. Montrose," the policeman replied. "Just kids fooling around, I guess. Do you know the Wilsons on Cherry Street? Mrs. Wilson called and said her Doug had been attacked by a gang near this house. Couldn't find any gang when I came, though. But I think I've figured out what happened, all except how these garden tools got out."

"I don't like the idea of anyone fooling around here," Mr. Montrose said. "Some of the men at the bank still think we have a chance of selling the house, and it won't help if we start getting broken windows and that sort of thing. This is Jack Aylesworth. He's just started to work at the bank, and he's going to try to sell the house."

"I'm sure we can sell a handsome place like this," the young man said. "These old houses are very popular when they're in good condition."

"You must be new in town as well as at the bank," Sergeant Markowitz said, "but that explains what was puzzling me. I didn't realize you were getting the place fixed up to sell. It's perfectly obvious what happened. Doug sneaked in to see what trouble he could get into, and he was so busy looking over his shoulder to see if anybody was watching that he tripped over the rake and landed on the hose and turned it on himself. I never saw a wetter boy. I'll just go back and tell Mrs. Wilson to keep her son out of other people's yards, and maybe you'd better tell the man who's doing your yard work to put his tools away at night."

Wilbur and Mortimer were trying hard not to laugh, because they wanted to stay and hear what the men had to say. Sergeant Markowitz got in his car and then leaned out the window to say, "I wish you luck selling the house, but you'd better find a stranger to buy it." He laughed and drove off.

Mr. Aylesworth said, "That's funny, Mr. Montrose. I thought you told me we'd look the place over tonight and then hire somebody to do whatever needed doing. I didn't know you had a man working here already."

"We don't," Mr. Montrose said. Wilbur thought he looked cross.

"The yard looks as if someone has been taking care of it," Mr. Aylesworth said. "The lawn is mowed, and I'm sure those bushes have been pruned. When you told me the house had been empty since 1929, I pictured an old place with peeling paint, broken windows, grass up to my knees."

"I suppose you'll have to know," Mr. Montrose said reluctantly. "The place is supposed to be haunted. The bank had a mortgage on it when the last owner died, and since nobody else in the family came forward to pay it, we were stuck with the house. I understand the bank tried hard to sell it, but all the people who came to look at it were scared off. Then we more or less forgot about it for years, but last winter a new man in the mortgage department decided we ought to get rid of the place and stop paying taxes on it. I brought a real-estate agent to look it over, but he was scared away, and none of the other agents in town will touch it. I'd just as soon give it to the village Historical Society, but I agreed to try selling it one more time."

Wilbur and Mortimer waited to hear Mr. Aylesworth say he wasn't going to be scared away by a silly ghost story, but he surprised them. He asked, "Is the house really haunted, Mr. Montrose? I wonder what caused it. Was there a murder, do you know? Do people see the ghosts, or do they only hear noises? Do you know whether . . ."

85

"There certainly wasn't a murder," Mr. Montrose snapped. "The Temples were one of the finest families in Templeton. Don't be ridiculous. You aren't going to tell me you believe in ghosts, are you?"

"You have to keep an open mind about these things," Mr. Aylesworth said solemnly. "One of my professors at college was very interested in hauntings. I think I'll write to him tonight and ask if he wouldn't like to investigate this house. Could we go inside? I'd like to be able to tell him all about the house; and if I should be fortunate enough to hear anything, I could describe it for him."

"Don't you think you might be scared off too?" Mr. Montrose suggested.

"I think you're making fun of me," Mr. Aylesworth said. "Of course I wouldn't be frightened, because I know what to expect. First it gets very cold, and you get a feeling something is about to happen. Then if you're lucky you hear noises, usually footsteps, but sometimes it's rappings. If you're very lucky you see a sort of shimmer, like a piece of cellophane, and if you're very, very lucky the ghosts may even speak. They want to communicate with people, but not everyone is sympathetic enough to hear them. I imagine they'd be quite glad to see someone who isn't afraid of them."

"I never heard anything so ridiculous," Mr. Montrose said. He was remembering the day in February when he had been at the house. He had felt cold, all right, but he expected to feel cold in an unheated house in February, and certainly none of the Temples had reminded him of cellophane.

Mortimer and Wilbur were laughing so much that they had to drift into the house. They told their parents that Mr. Montrose was in the yard with a new man from the bank who wanted to see some ghosts. "He's going to investigate us," Mortimer said, "and he thinks we'll look like cellophane."

"That's ridiculous," Mr. Temple said.

"That's what Mr. Montrose said," Wilbur told him.

"We didn't put the tools away," Mr. Temple said. "You and that Wilson boy drove it right out of my mind. Suppose we finish cleaning up the yard, and maybe we can show this man a thing or two at the same time."

They drifted out to the yard as Mr. Montrose and Mr. Aylesworth were coming around the corner of the house. "Somebody really did leave tools out," Mr. Aylesworth said. "I wonder who."

"Maybe a ghost," Mr. Montrose snapped.

Mr. Aylesworth laughed. "I'm afraid not, Mr. Montrose," he said. "That isn't the sort of thing ghosts do. They're trying to get revenge, or right a wrong, or something like that. They don't do yard work. Why should they?"

Just then he saw the wheelbarrow come around the other side of the house. It rolled toward a large compost heap at the far end of the yard, stood itself up, and dumped a pile of clippings and weeds on top of the heap. Then it turned around and rolled away. At the same time, a hoe that had been lying near a flower bed rose into the air and floated across the yard toward a shed. The shed door opened, the hoe went inside, and the door banged shut. Then it bounced open again. "Darn it," said Wilbur, "I wish Dad would fix that latch." The door shut itself gently, and this time it stayed closed.

Mr. Aylesworth stood with his mouth open, looking very foolish. "What was that?" he asked at last.

"One of your ghosts perhaps," Mr. Montrose suggested again.

"It couldn't be," Mr. Aylesworth said faintly. "That isn't at all the sort of thing ghosts do."

Mr. Montrose said, "Don't forget, it's important to keep an open mind, Jack." He pointed to where a hose was lying near the back door, with most of it stretched around to the side yard. While the men watched, the hose began to coil itself up, exactly as if someone were pulling it. Then it stopped, and they heard Mortimer say, "Darn, it's caught on something. Go see what it is, Wilbur."

A rake floated right by Mr. Aylesworth's ear and dropped in front of him. The hose jiggled up and down as if someone were trying to work it loose. In a minute Wilbur said, "Okay, it was caught in the rose bush. Now pull." The hose gave a great heave and the nozzle came flying around the corner of the house, straight for the two men. Wilbur shouted, "Look out, you'll hit somebody!" and Mr. Aylesworth jumped out of the way and landed on the rake. The handle bounced up and hit him on the back of the head so he lost his balance and fell on the hose. Mortimer gave it another good tug and rolled Mr. Aylesworth off so he could finish coiling it up. Mr. Aylesworth lay there, looking silly, until Mr. Montrose told him to get up.

"What's happening?" he asked. He tried to stand up and groaned.

"Now what?" Mr. Montrose asked.

"My ankle," Mr. Aylesworth moaned. "It's weak, and I keep spraining it. This is the second time this year."

"Now you've done it, Mortimer," Wilbur said. "What'll we do?"

"Get Dad," Mortimer said uneasily. "Gosh, I'm sorry, Mr. Aylesworth. I didn't mean to hurt you."

The wheelbarrow came round the side of the house again, with another load of clippings. When Mortimer called his father, it rolled over to where Mr. Aylesworth was stretched out on the ground and said, "What's the matter? Is this the man who wanted to investigate us?"

Mr. Aylesworth shut his eyes and moaned again. Mr. Montrose said, "I wish now we hadn't decided to walk. I don't know how we'll get you home, and I suppose we really ought to take you to a doctor."

"We could take him inside and send for a doctor," Mr. Temple suggested. "I could send Mortimer."

"You might send him," Mr. Montrose said, "but I doubt if the doctor would come. If an invisible boy started telling me to come here and treat a sprained ankle, I'd treat myself first."

"I could appear," Mortimer said, and immediately stood before them in his school clothes.

"You ought to sit up and take a look at this, Jack," Mr. Montrose said. "Here's one of your ghosts in the flesh."

Mr. Aylesworth cautiously opened his eyes and

90

looked at Mortimer. Then he sat up and said, "You're making fun of me again, Mr. Montrose. Is this the boy who's been throwing the tools around? He ought to be ashamed, and I don't think you should encourage him, Mr. Montrose, pretending to think he's a ghost like that. I know what ghosts look like. They're either transparent, or they appear in the clothes they were wearing when they died."

"Do you like this better?" Mortimer asked. He vanished and returned dressed in the clothes that were fashionable ninety years before. Then he vanished again and appeared in his bones. He had been

practicing that for some time, and was very proud of his success because it was much harder than clothes. Finally he appeared in a long white garment like a large bag. "My haunting clothes," he explained. "What do you think of them?"

Mr. Aylesworth lay back down and shut his eyes again. He moaned faintly and said, "Maybe my ankle is broken this time."

"Don't forget to keep an open mind," Mr. Montrose said.

Before anything else could happen, Wilbur said, "Here's Mother. She'll know what to do."

"I'm surprised at you," Mrs. Temple said. "Bring that poor young man in the house before he gets a chill. Imagine leaving him on this cold ground so long."

Mr. Aylesworth felt himself picked up and carried into the house. He screamed faintly, but Mr. Montrose, who was walking along behind him, didn't seem at all upset. The Temples laid Mr. Aylesworth gently on the couch, and Mr. Temple asked if he had fainted.

"His pulse is steady, and he's breathing all right," Mrs. Temple replied. "I think we'd better give him a little tonic to revive him. Open your eyes, Mr. Aylesworth, and drink this. You'll feel better."

When Mr. Aylesworth opened his eyes, he couldn't see anyone but Mr. Montrose. A glass floated toward him and he shut his eyes again. "I'll pour it on you if you don't drink it," Mrs. Temple warned him. "What's the matter with him, Mr.

Montrose? I thought he wanted to see some ghosts."

"You're the wrong kind," said Mr. Montrose, who seemed to be quite cheerful now. "He knows just what a ghost should look like, and you don't conform. He thinks if this house is haunted, it's because of a murder and you're supposed to look like cellophane. You should make the room turn cold, too."

"I never heard such nonsense," Mrs. Temple said briskly. "We were struck by lightning, and it all happened so quickly we wound up ghosts. That's all there is to it. Now sit up and drink this and stop acting like a baby, Mr. Aylesworth. I'm sorry you hurt your ankle, but I'm sure we can get you home without any trouble. Come on now."

Mr. Aylesworth continued to lie still with his eyes shut tight. He heard Mortimer say, "If he knew my mother better, he'd know she doesn't just threaten," and felt something wet running down his chin.

"Fellow's a nincompoop," Mr. Montrose said. "I knew it all along. But he was our last hope when it came to selling this house. You can see that we have to do something, can't you?"

"The first thing you have to do is take this young man home," Mrs. Temple said.

"How?" Mr. Montrose asked. "I really don't think he can walk."

"I'll tell you," Mrs. Temple replied.

A few minutes later, Sergeant Markowitz was driving down Oak Street on his regular patrol. He looked at the Temple House, as he always did, and saw that it looked deserted as usual. He shook his head and drove on, but in the next block he saw something so odd that he stopped the car to take a closer look. Mr. Montrose was walking down the sidewalk, talking to someone, and beside him a wheelbarrow was rolling along. No one was pushing it, but the young man who had been with Mr. Montrose at the Temple House was sitting in it with his legs dangling over the side and his eyes tight shut.

Sergeant Markowitz got out and asked Mr. Mont-

rose if he could do anything for him. Mr. Aylesworth opened his eyes a crack and said, "Police. Thank heaven. I've been attacked. Take me to a doctor."

The back door of the police car swung open and Mr. Aylesworth floated from the wheelbarrow to the back seat. The door slammed shut. Sergeant Markowitz said, "He can't be too badly hurt. He got in the car fast enough. What happened to him, Mr. Montrose? Was he really attacked?"

"My ankle," Mr. Aylesworth moaned. "Take me to a doctor."

"He fell over the rake at the Temple House and sprained his ankle," Mr. Montrose said. "There's no phone in that house, and he didn't seem to want to stay there alone while I walked home to get my car, so I brought him along in the wheelbarrow."

"The same rake?" Sergeant Markowitz asked. Mr. Montrose nodded. "Twice in one evening is too much," Sergeant Markowitz said. "It's enough to make a person wonder if . . . I think I'll go back and take another look."

"I wouldn't bother," Mr. Montrose said. "We didn't see a living soul. If you could just take him to the doctor, it would be a help."

"Get in," Sergeant Markowitz sighed. "I'll take you home too." He drove off quickly, being careful not to look in the rear-view mirrow. If the wheelbarrow was taking itself home, he didn't want to see it.

Mortimer
Takes
Music

"GUESS WHAT?" Mortimer said to his parents one night. "Mr. Angell came to all the classes and said the band needs more people, and he'll give lessons to anyone who wants to learn a band instrument. He said that anyone who already knew how to play the piano could probably learn to play something else. I sure wish I could be in the band. You should see the new uniforms."

"Why shouldn't you?" his mother asked. "I think that would be very nice. Maybe Wilbur would like to, too."

"Not me," Wilbur said, "but it might be nice for Mortimer to play in it."

"Maybe I will, if you think it's all right," Mortimer said.

The next morning when they were drifting to school, Wilbur asked, "Are you really going to try to join the band? You know what Mother said would happen if we caused any more disturbance at school."

"You heard her last night," Mortimer reminded him. "She said it would be nice if I took music. Can I help it if I do something she thinks would be nice and there's a disturbance?"

Later that morning, Mr. Graham was coming out of his office when he heard a drum being played very badly in the music room at the other end of the hall. He saw that the door had been left open again, and hurried down the hall to shut it, but before he got there the drumming stopped. Mr. Graham listened a minute and heard a hair-raising squawk from some kind of horn and then the crash of cymbals. Just as he reached the door, the piano began to play. Whoever the person was, he could play the piano well enough for Mr. Graham to recognize "America the Beautiful," but Mr. Graham still felt that he must tell whoever it was that he ought to have the door closed. As he was about to enter the room, Mr. Graham saw Mr. Angell come out of the supply room with a pile of notebooks and went to meet him. "Mr. Angell," he said firmly, "you'll have to remember to shut your door when you leave the music room. Your piano pupil was fooling around with the drums while you were out, and I could hear it way down in my office."

"There wasn't anyone in the room when I left," Mr. Angell said. "I don't have a class this period, but the sixth-grade flutes are due in five minutes.

Maybe one of them is early." Both men heard the piano start to play "Yankee Doodle," and they looked in the room, but there was no one there. They could see the piano keys sinking and bobbing up again, and they could hear "Yankee Doodle," but the piano stool was definitely empty.

"Oh no, not again!" Mr. Graham sighed. But Mr. Angell paid no attention.

"How very ingenious," he said. "Some sort of electronic device, no doubt. Do you notice, Mr. Graham, that there is no one here?" Mr. Graham nodded weakly. "Isn't it clever?" Mr. Angell beamed. "It must be a science project. I must congratulate Mr. Humphrey, I really must. I expect someone is playing the auditorium piano and there are wires. Yes, I think there would have to be wires somewhere, don't you, Mr. Graham? Or maybe not. I don't really understand these things. But isn't it clever?"

Just then a bell rang and the piano stopped playing. "What a shame," Mr. Angell went on. "Now my sixth-grade flutes will be coming, and no doubt the person who is playing the auditorium piano has another class too."

Several children with instrument cases rushed into the room, and Mr. Angell backed out of the way. "Would you care to stay and hear the flutes, Mr. Graham?" he asked. "No? Well, perhaps you're wise, but they really are improving. If you happen to pass the science room, you might tell Mr.

Humphrey that his device is a complete success. Really remarkable."

Mr. Graham walked on down the hall, shaking his head doubtfully, and Mr. Angell entered the music room, being careful to latch the door. The children had put their music on the stands and were holding their flutes, ready to begin playing.

"Let's try 'Marching Along' first," Mr. Angell said. "All together when I give you the count." After they had played a few bars, he said, "Stop. If you make a mistake, just keep going. If everybody who makes a mistake says 'oh dear' and goes back to correct a wrong note, we can't possibly keep together. Try it again from the beginning, and go straight to the end, no matter what happens." When they had played it all the way through, Mr. Angell said, "Jerry, you have not been practicing. Your timing is off. Listen while I play it on the piano."

He opened the music book that was on the piano; but before he could strike a note, the piano began to play "Marching Along." The class stared and Jerry said, "Gosh, Mr. Angell, how did you do that?"

"I bet it's . . ." a girl began; but Mr. Angell said, "The science class has made a remote-control device that plays our piano."

"How could the science class know you'd want 'Marching Along' just then?" the girl asked.

"Never mind, Eileen, let's try it again, all together. Watch your timing, Jerry." The flutes played, and the piano accompanied them. "Much better," Mr. Angell said. "The piano helps, doesn't it? Of course you won't have a piano in a parade."

"Aren't we ever going to get a new piece?" another girl asked. "I'm getting tired of 'Marching Along.'"

"You all need to practice this one some more," Mr. Angell said, "but I want you to start learning the next one, too. Look at the music while I play it for you. Or maybe our piano would like to try it?" The piano played the next piece while the children stared. "I don't think you were all watching the music," Mr. Angell said. "Try it. Without the piano please," he added, and the piano obediently stopped playing. When they had each played the new piece, Mr. Angell said, "You'll have to put your flutes away now; it's time for the percussion class, but don't forget to practice."

Eileen said, "I bet I know who played the piano. My sister's in the third grade and she says . . ."

"You'll be late for your next class if you stay here talking, Eileen. Good-bye," Mr. Angell said.

When the percussion class came in, Mortimer recognized Janie Snodgrass and Jimmy Falcon. There was a fat boy named Clarence, too, and a tall girl with long black hair, and a couple of other boys. As soon as they were in the room, Clarence said, "Guess what, Mr. Angell? Eleanor's mother called my mother this morning and said Eleanor had to have her appendix out in the middle of the night last night. She went to the hospital in the ambulance, and she won't be back for at least two weeks — maybe more. Gee, I hope she told them to save it so she can bring it to school in a bottle. That would be keen."

"Our only glockenspiel," Mr. Angell said. "What a pity. I'm afraid we won't sound the same without her. I wish our pianist could play the glockenspiel too, but I suppose that's too much to hope for."

"I don't even know what the thing looks like," Mortimer said, "but I'll be glad to try."

"What was that?" gasped a couple of boys. "Did you hear that, Mr. Angell?" Everybody else just stared.

"That's Mr. Humphrey's new invention," Mr. Angell explained. "Isn't it clever? He's made something so someone can play the piano in our room from another room, and I think there must be an intercom with it."

"That's funny, he never told our class about it," Jimmy said.

"Perhaps he was saving it for a surprise," Mr. Angell said. "Would you play something for us, piano?" The piano obligingly played "Twinkle, Twinkle, Little Star."

"You see, it works," Mr. Angell told them happily, "but I'm afraid it really can't play the glockenspiel. Never mind, a piano will be better than nothing. Much better," he added, so the piano's feelings wouldn't be hurt.

"You could at least show me the thing," a voice said. "How do I know if I can play it if I don't even know what it looks like?"

Clarence, who was standing by a big drum, said, "It's that thing with the little bars. I tried to learn it once, but I wasn't very good. I'm better with the drums."

"Much better," Mr. Angell agreed. "Let's begin."

The little hammer jumped up from beside the glockenspiel and began hitting the bars one by one. "Hey, that's neat!" Mortimer exclaimed. "I like this."

There was a reverberating crash, and Mr. Angell looked around. He had been staring at the glockenspiel, wondering how the hammer could hit the bars when nothing was holding it, and now he saw that a tall girl had turned pale and was trembling so violently that she had dropped her cymbals. He picked them up and said, "You must be careful not to drop them, Noreen. You aren't ill, are you?"

"It's the little people," Noreen whispered. "My grandmother used to see them in the old country. Oh dear, oh dear."

"Nonsense," Mr. Angell snapped. "You know

there aren't any little people — at least not in America. It's just some kind of electronic gadget."

"Look at that," Jimmy squeaked. Mr. Angell looked and saw a music book float across the room. It hovered beside another book for a second, then opened itself and set itself down in front of the glockenspiel. "Now if I just knew which note was which, we could all play together," Mortimer said.

"Maybe if you'd read the first page, it would tell you," Janie suggested. She was standing near the door, and there were two drummers and a big boy with cymbals between her and the glockenspiel, so she felt quite safe. Anyway, she was pretty sure she knew who was talking.

"Thank you," Mortimer said, and everyone saw the pages of the book flip back to the first page. "Here we are, I'll try a scale."

"Mr. Angell," Jimmy said, "I don't believe Mr. Humphrey could do all that, do you? Anyway, he's got eighth-grade science this period, and they're dissecting a grasshopper. He couldn't do this and dissect a grasshopper too, could he? You want to know what I think? Do you remember the time we had the gym rehearsal? Gosh, I'll never forget that."

Another boy laughed. "Remember the way you turned a somersault over the horse, Jimmy? I bet Mr. O'Reilly still thinks you could do it again if you'd just try."

"Not me," Jimmy said with a grin. "Anyway, I bet this is the same person. That's what I bet."

The other children were standing there staring

while the hammer played scales on the glockenspiel and the voice murmured, "A, B, C, D, E, F, G, F, E, D, C, B, A." All but Noreen, who was sitting down with her hands over her face, moaning.

"This really is remarkable," Mr. Angell said, "but I'm sure there's some explanation." The bell rang and he said, "Oh dear, I'm afraid we haven't learned much this period. Be sure to practice, and I'll see you tomorrow."

"Not me," said Noreen. "I'm never coming back." She ran out the door so fast that she bumped into Mr. Graham, who was on his way in.

He looked at her in surprise. "What's the matter, Noreen? Have you been crying?"

Before she could reply, Mr. Angell stuck his head out the door and said, "Noreen was frightened by Mr. Humphrey's new invention. She thought it was the little people, but I told her not to be afraid. It can't possibly hurt anyone."

Mr. Graham wiped his forehead and said, "This school is bewitched. No, no, Noreen, I didn't really mean it," he added impatiently when Noreen began to sniff again. "You run along now."

He stepped into the room and turned to Mr. Angell. "Did you have more trouble this period?"

"No, no," said Mr. Angell. "Though these new inventions are unsettling, I must admit. I just don't understand how they work. I must thank Mr. Humphrey for his help on the piano, but I think I'll have to tell him that he doesn't do as well on the glockenspiel."

The
Practice
Teacher

THE NEXT DAY Mr. Graham stepped in to see Miss
Hartley. He found the class giving oral book re-
ports. When Miss Hartley invited him to sit down
and listen, he said, "I'm afraid I don't have time
today. I have an announcement. You will have a
young woman in here helping Miss Hartley for a
few weeks. She's learning to be a teacher, and she's
going to practice some of the things she's learned
and watch an experienced teacher at work. Some
of you may know her because her family lives on
Spring Street. Her name is Miss Morrison, and her
father is the president of our school board."

He lowered his voice and said to Miss Hartley,
"I really didn't want to give this room to a practice
teacher, but she wants primary, and this is the only
primary room that hasn't been assigned. Of course

106

I couldn't refuse to have her, but I wish she didn't have to be in this room. I know you haven't had any trouble lately, but every time I come in here I expect something to happen. You will . . . I mean you don't think . . . well, we certainly don't want our school to get a bad reputation, do we?"

"We'll do the best we can to make her happy, won't we, class?" Miss Hartley assured him. "When is she coming, Mr. Graham?"

"Monday. Be careful with her, won't you?" Mr. Graham looked a little anxious and then left.

Miss Hartley smiled at the children and said, "It's only a few years since I was practice-teaching, and I don't know whether I was more scared of the teacher or the children. Please be nice to her. At least don't treat her like a substitute. And please, Wilbur, don't scare her."

Louise bounced in her chair and said, "Miss Hartley, if her father finds out we have a ghost in our class, what will happen? Something awful, I bet."

"That will do, Louise," Miss Hartley said. "And please raise your hand." She took a magazine out of her desk and said, "We have just time for me to show you these pictures. My brother and a friend of his took some pictures of Wilbur's house last Christmas vacation, and they were quite surprised when they looked at the pictures and saw Wilbur and his family. My brother's friend sent the pictures to an architecture magazine that was having a contest for pictures of old houses, and they won third prize."

107

"Gosh," Alan said. "Wilbur will be famous, with his picture in a magazine. Let's see."

"I'll pass it around," Miss Hartley said. "Wilbur, the article with the pictures says your house is for sale. What will your family do if somebody buys it? Will you stay there?"

"My father says . . ." Wilbur began.

"Please appear, Wilbur," Miss Hartley interrupted him. "I haven't seen you since roll call. And do try to stay visible while Miss Morrison is here. I know it will be hard for you, but it will help us all."

Wilbur appeared and said, "I'll try, Miss Hartley. About the house, my father says he thinks he and Mr. Montrose can work something out."

Before Miss Hartley could ask him any more questions, the bell rang for dismissal.

"Have a nice weekend, everybody," Miss Hartley said. "Don't forget to be good to our practice teacher next week, and Wilbur, maybe you could practice appearing this weekend."

When Miss Morrison came on Monday morning, she turned out to be very quiet and pretty. She wore her hair wound up in a curl on top of her head, and she wore glasses on a chain around her neck and put them on whenever she wanted to look across the room. She came right after opening exercises, and at first Miss Hartley just let her sit in the visitor's chair and watch. In the afternoon Miss Hartley said, "Now that you've seen the class a little, suppose we introduce ourselves. Where do you go to college, Miss Morrison?"

Miss Morrison said, "I go to State University, but my home is right here in town. My family lives on Spring Street, and my father is a lawyer."

She couldn't seem to think of anything else to say, so Miss Hartley asked each member of the class to stand up and introduce himself. When it was Wilbur's turn, she held her breath, but he stood up and said, "My name is Wilbur Temple and I live on Oak Street." So far, Wilbur had been visible all day, and she hoped he wouldn't vanish when they did arithmetic.

While the class was busy with arithmetic, Miss Hartley started to show Miss Morrison what they were doing; but Kathy raised her hand and said, "I don't get this, Miss Hartley."

"What don't you understand, Kathy?" Miss Hartley asked.

"Well, it says here that if you keep subtracting 6 from this number, you find out how many times 6 goes into it. I don't get it."

"Show her, Wilbur," Miss Hartley said automatically. Then she saw that Wilbur had disappeared, as he always did when he was thinking hard, and she said, "I'm sorry, Miss Morrison. I'm not used to having a helper yet. Maybe you'd like to explain it to Kathy. Wilbur is so good at explaining arithmetic that I'm afraid I've gotten in the habit of asking him to do it."

By this time Wilbur had appeared beside Kathy's

desk. Miss Morrison said, "I'd like to hear how he explains it. I might learn something too." Miss Hartley looked at her, but she saw that Miss Morrison wasn't wearing her glasses and hoped that she hadn't noticed anything unusual.

Wilbur explained very thoroughly, and at last Kathy said, "Now I see. Thank you, Wilbur."

On Mondays after arithmetic they always had singing. Miss Hartley was a little nervous about it because Wilbur could never carry a tune without vanishing, but she thought it would be safer to stick to the schedule than to try to explain why she didn't. He did vanish once, but Miss Morrison was looking dreamily out of the window.

Music was the last period on Monday, and Miss Hartley congratulated herself that they had gotten through one day without disaster. She whispered to Wilbur as he went out the door, "Thank you, Wilbur. Keep it up."

Wilbur whispered back, "I'll try, but it's awfully hard. Do you think it would be better if I stayed home?"

Miss Hartley said, "Don't worry. Of course not. Just whatever you do, don't throw any goldfish bowls at her."

After a week, Miss Hartley began to think nothing would go wrong. Miss Morrison was a little bashful, but even a very bashful person would mention it if she saw a ghost in school. Wilbur was trying very hard to be visible all the time, and whenever he forgot, Miss Morrison either didn't have her

glasses on or was looking at something else. Furthermore, the whole class was so anxious to keep Wilbur and Miss Hartley out of trouble that they were behaving with superhuman goodness. Miss Hartley thought there hadn't been such a good class since the school was built.

One chilly day Miss Hartley asked Miss Morrison to take the class out for recess while she stayed in and drank a cup of tea, because she thought she was catching a cold. Recess seemed safe because the whole school went out at once, and Miss Morrison couldn't possibly be sure Wilbur wasn't there. Miss Morrison came in a few minutes early and said, "Wow! I hope I never get William Snodgrass angry with me."

"William?" Miss Hartley said. "Why, I've always thought he was a peaceable boy. What happened?"

"His little sister came out with her class, all bundled up, and Doug Wilson — I think that's his name, that fat boy from the fifth grade who's always picking on people — anyway, he started to chase her and told William she ran like a hippopotamus. I don't see how a little boy like William could do it, but he beat Doug up good and proper. It almost looked as if someone were holding Doug while William hit him, and every time Doug tried to hit William, his arm jerked back so he couldn't. It was the craziest thing I ever saw. Finally Mr. O'Reilly saw what was going on and came over and told Doug to pick on someone his own size. You should have seen his face when he saw that Doug had a black eye and a puffy nose and William wasn't even scratched. I brought them in before anything else could happen, but I made them stop in the hall to take their boots off. That's right, isn't it?"

"Quite right," Miss Hartley said faintly. "Here they come."

When the class came in, Miss Hartley saw Wilbur look nervously at Miss Morrison, but the wind had blown her curl down and she was so busy pinning it up that she didn't pay any attention to Wilbur.

The next day Miss Hartley called and said she had the flu, so Miss Morrison had to teach the class alone for several days. The second day she was alone with the class, Ann's hamster got loose while she was cleaning the cage. All the children scurried around the room, trying to catch it, but the hamster got between the bookcase and the wall, where no one could reach him. Ann began to cry. "He'll starve," she sobbed. "Or someone will open the door and he'll sneak out and I'll never find him again. What'll we do?"

Everybody looked hopefully at Wilbur.

Miss Morrison said, "Suppose we all sit down quietly and shut our eyes and think. Maybe some-one will think of a way to get him back. Ann, you sit by the bookcase and watch. Maybe he'll come out if we stop making so much noise." Miss Morrison put her head down on the desk and shut her eyes.

Wilbur drifted across the room and through the bookcase. He grasped the hamster gently and whispered, "Here, Ann, I think I've got him where you can reach him now."

Ann glanced at Miss Morrison, but her eyes were still shut. She took the hamster and put it back in its cage. Wilbur drifted back to his seat and appeared again. Ann said, "It worked, Miss Morrison. I got him back."

Miss Morrison said it was always better to stop and think about a problem than to rush around making a lot of noise.

When Miss Hartley came back, she still looked a little pale, but she said she felt fine. She asked what the class had been doing while she was away. Miss Morrison said she hoped they had done what Miss Hartley wanted them to. "We read the story about the princess on the glass hill and drew pictures of it for you. See them on the bulletin board."

"They look very nice," Miss Hartley said. "What else did you do?"

Ann raised her hand and said, "We did the practice test in spelling yesterday, and Wilbur got all his words right. Didn't he, Miss Morrison?"

"Yes, he did. We were proud of him. And we studied some more about pioneers in the social studies book. I read the children a chapter from *Little House on the Prairie*. I wanted the class to draw maps of the pioneer trails for their notebooks, but I couldn't find a good one for them to look at first."

"There's a big one in the storeroom, I think," Miss Hartley said. "I'll get it. That would be a good project for this morning. Did anything else happen while I was away?"

"Nothing to speak of," Miss Morrison said.

Miss Hartley got out the map, and after a little trouble, the teachers managed to hang it over the blackboard so everyone could see it. When the children had finished drawing their maps, Miss

Morrison said maybe they should put the big map away, but Miss Hartley said the janitor could do it after school.

In the afternoon, Miss Morrison asked if they could have a spelling bee. Miss Hartley thought this was a good idea, too, so they lined the girls up in front of the windows and the boys in front of the blackboard. Just as they were ready to start, a big man with gray hair came in. Miss Morrison said, "Why, hello, Dad, what are you doing here?" Everybody looked at Wilbur, but he was standing quietly with the other boys.

The man said, "I had a few minutes before my next appointment and I wanted to see how you were getting along. I hope you don't mind?"

Miss Hartley said they were glad to see him and gave him the visitor's chair. She handed Miss Morrison the spelling book and sat down at her desk. At first everybody spelled the words right. Then Bobby missed "president" and sat down, so the girls were ahead. Now Wilbur was getting nervous. He was a terrible speller anyway, and he couldn't concentrate without vanishing. The boy before him missed "entirely" but Kathy spelled it right. Miss Morrison said, "Your word is 'go,' Wilbur."

Wilbur said, "G-O, go," and everybody sighed with relief.

Mr. Morrison said, "That's an awfully easy word, isn't it?" but Miss Morrison told him she liked to put an easy one in once in a while. Several girls went down after that, so the boys were ahead. Jason was getting so excited he kept teetering back and forth on his heels. Miss Hartley asked him twice to stop, but he kept doing it until finally he went back too far and hit the blackboard with such a smack that the big map fell down on top of Wilbur. Wilbur was so surprised he vanished. Miss Hartley jumped up, but Miss Morrison walked over and picked the map up. She said calmly, "Did it knock you down, Wilbur? Pull yourself together and get up. You aren't really hurt, are you?"

She rolled the map up and stood it in the corner. Everybody saw Wilbur get up off the floor and dust himself off.

Mr. Morrison said, "I never heard of anyone's falling down without making a noise. How did you do it, boy?"

Wilbur mumbled, "I guess I fell slowly."

Mr. Morrison had to leave after that, and his daughter walked down the hall with him. Willie said, "Boy, are we lucky! How come she didn't notice you weren't there? She was looking right at you."

Wilbur said, "I guess she was looking at the map."

Louise bounced up and said, "Wilbur, do you want to get Miss Hartley in trouble? I knew we should have made you stay home while Miss Morrison was here."

"It was Jason's fault as much as Wilbur's," Willie shouted.

"Gosh, I didn't mean to knock it down," Jason said. "I'm sorry, Miss Hartley."

"Just don't teeter like that, Jason," Miss Hartley said.

Miss Morrison came back and asked if everything was all right. "I thought I'd better take Daddy to the car so he wouldn't stay talking all afternoon in the office. I think the boys won in spelling, don't you, Miss Hartley?"

A few days later Miss Morrison's last day came, so the class had a party for her with punch and cookies. At the end of the party, Miss Morrison said, "I've heard that one of the girls who was practice-teaching has decided not to teach after all, but I've loved being with you. There's just one thing I'd like — well, two, really."

"What are they?" Miss Hartley asked. Everybody was feeling relaxed and happy because Miss Morrison was so nice and they had kept their secret so well. They would have done anything for her.

Miss Morrison walked over to the bookcase and dropped an eraser down behind it. "I'd like to see Wilbur go through the bookcase and get that eraser," she said. "I had to keep my eyes shut when he got the hamster out."

Everybody gasped and stared, and no one said a word. At last Miss Hartley asked, "You mean you know? Why didn't you say anything?"

"Why didn't you?" Miss Morrison replied. "Please, Wilbur, won't you do it for a good-bye present for me?"

Wilbur looked at Miss Hartley and she nodded, so he walked over to the bookcase, disappeared,

drifted through it, shoved the eraser out along the floor, and reappeared. "The eraser won't go through the bookcase," he explained.

"Thank you, Wilbur," Miss Morrison said. "I wish I could do that."

Miss Hartley laughed till the tears rolled down her face. "To think that we've been congratulating ourselves for a month that you hadn't noticed anything strange," she gasped. "Oh dear, now I've got hiccups. And poor Wilbur is getting quite thin from the strain of being visible all the time. How long have you known?" A glass of water floated across the room to her and she drank it and said, "Thank you, Wilbur."

"I saw Wilbur disappear the first day I was here," Miss Morrison said. "I may be a little nearsighted, but I can tell an empty space from a boy any time. I was surprised at first, but I could tell that everybody in the class was used to him and trying not to let me know, so I made up my mind that I'd get used to him too. By the way, I heard Mr. Angell saying something about a marvelous gadget the science class has invented that plays the piano by remote control, and he says he's teaching it to play the glockenspiel, too. Is that you, Wilbur?"

"That's my brother, Mortimer," Wilbur replied. "He'd like to be in the band, but Mr. Angell doesn't believe in ghosts. He's sure Mortimer is a scientific marvel, and he calls him 'Piano,' because the first time Mortimer was there he played the piano. It makes Mortimer awfully mad."

"Oh dear," Miss Morrison said. "I never thought a ghost would have a problem with people who didn't believe in ghosts. Poor Mortimer. What's he going to do?"

"He doesn't know," Wilbur told her.

"What was the other thing you wanted?" Miss Hartley asked. "It's almost time to go home, but if it's something quick we could manage it."

"Oh, I've just been wondering how Wilbur gets his clothes," Miss Morrison explained. "I keep thinking of the uproar there'd be in the men's shop if an invisible woman was trying clothes on an invisible little boy, but of course he wouldn't have to be invisible, would he?"

"That would be fun," Wilbur grinned.

"Show her, Wilbur," Willie said. "It's neat, Miss Morrison."

Wilbur vanished and appeared in his old-fashioned clothes. He vanished again and reappeared in a blouse and skirt, with white ankle socks and red sandals like Nina's. Finally he appeared in his school clothes, with his outdoor jacket on.

"That's wonderful," Miss Morrison said. "I wish I didn't have to leave, but it's time. I'll visit you the next time I'm in Templeton. Good-bye. Don't forget me."

Miss Hartley
Goes
Calling

ONE DAY IN MAY, Miss Hartley said, "Class, I need your help. Mr. Graham has decided that this year's play should be a pageant about the history of Templeton, and he's asked Mr. Martin and me to write it. I think he should have picked somebody else, because I've only lived here a short time and Mr. Martin hasn't been here much longer. Do you know whose family has been in Templeton a long time and could tell us about the early days here?"

Ann raised her hand and said, "It could start with the Pilgrims landing."

"In Ohio?" Jason asked.

Wilbur appeared and raised his hand.

"Yes, Wilbur?"

"My mother and father know a lot about Templeton, Miss Hartley. My father was the first baby born in Templeton, and he's lived here ever since. If you could come to my house, he'd tell you a lot."

"Thank you, Wilbur," Miss Hartley said. "I'd love to meet your parents. Suppose you ask them when it would be convenient for me to visit them. I think your mother and father would be the perfect people to help me."

That evening Wilbur told his parents about the pageant, and they said he could bring Miss Hartley home after school whenever she wanted to come.

"Tell her to bring a lot of paper," Mortimer said. "If Dad has a new audience, he'll talk all night."

"Don't be rude, Mortimer," his mother said.

"The band is going to play, too," Mortimer said quickly, before his mother could say any more about manners. "Mr. Angell was talking about it today. I wish he'd get another glockenspiel, so Eleanor and I could both play."

"Does Mr. Angell still think you're a gadget?" his father asked.

"I'm afraid so. He still calls me 'Piano.' Janie says I should appear for him, but Jimmy Falcon says he's so proud of his gadget that the disappointment might give him a heart attack or something. Maybe I can be in the play if I can't be in the band. Could I?"

"We could ask Miss Hartley," Wilbur said doubtfully. "It would be better if you'd appear in school instead of just fooling around. Mr. Martin will be kind of surprised to see a student he's never heard of in the play, won't he?"

"You ask Miss Hartley," Mortimer said. "She'll figure out something. It's a good thing it's Mr. Martin and not Mr. Humphrey."

"Why?" his mother asked.

"I've never been in Mr. Martin's class," Mortimer explained. "I don't think Mr. Humphrey likes me since the day he was telling the science class about the human skeleton and I appeared in my bones. Everybody screamed, and one girl fainted. It was a lot of fun."

"Mortimer, I've told you . . ." his mother began, but before she could say what she had told him, Mr. Temple said they had better think about what they would tell Miss Hartley.

The next day after school, Miss Hartley walked home with Wilbur. Even though she was very fond of Wilbur, she was a little nervous about going to a haunted house, and Wilbur made her even more nervous because he was so excited he kept vanishing.

When they got to the house, Miss Hartley said, "I've always wanted to see the inside of this house." Wilbur drifted through the gate, but then he came back and opened it for Miss Hartley. She thought the house didn't really look haunted. The paint was fresh, the lawn had just been mowed, and there was a big flower bed in the front yard.

The door swung open, and Wilbur said, "Come in, Miss Hartley." Miss Hartley walked in, and the door closed behind her.

Miss Hartley thought it didn't really look haunted

inside, either. There was no dust or cobwebs, and although the furniture looked old, it was well polished and attractive. She did wish she could see someone, though.

Wilbur said, "Here are my parents. Mother and Daddy, this is my teacher, Miss Hartley. Here's Mortimer, too. You've seen him, haven't you?"

Miss Hartley said, "How do you do?" in a very small voice.

A pleasant voice said, "How do you do, Miss Hartley? It's nice of you to call. We're delighted to meet Wilbur's teacher."

Then a man's voice said, "Shall we go in the parlor and sit down?" Miss Hartley saw the parlor through the doorway and moved slowly toward it.

Then Mortimer appeared and said, "For goodness sake, let her see you. You're scaring her to death."

Mrs. Temple said, "I'm so sorry, Miss Hartley. We aren't used to having company." Miss Hartley looked toward the voice and saw a woman with dark red hair pulled smoothly back from her face. She was wearing a long, full-skirted dress, and Miss Hartley thought she looked like an illustration for *Little Women*. Then a man appeared, and he was wearing old-fashioned clothes too.

Mortimer said, "I wish you'd wear modern clothes." But his mother said, "I've told you, Mortimer, I just can't get used to the idea of appearing in a short skirt."

"You look very nice," Miss Hartley told her. "I

wish I could put you in the pageant, just as you are."

Mrs. Temple immediately vanished and said, "Oh no, I couldn't be in a pageant."

"Don't worry," Miss Hartley said. "Only the schoolchildren will be in it; please come back."

Mrs. Temple slowly reappeared and said, "I'm sorry. Tell us about the pageant."

Miss Hartley told them what Mr. Graham wanted. "I don't know why he asked Mr. Martin and me to write it," she said. "There must be teachers who know more about Templeton than we do. I did go to a series of lectures last year though, right after I moved here. A Miss Bram gave them. Do you know her? I think she said her grandfather was the first mayor of Templeton, or was it her great-grandfather? Anyway, she made it sound as if the Brams invented Templeton. I was almost surprised that it wasn't called Bramville."

"It almost was," Mr. Temple told her. "I'll tell you what happened. My father and Lucius Bram brought their families here in 1839. This was all woods then. The first year it was a struggle to find enough to eat and to build a cabin to live in, but then things improved. This was a good location, with the river for water power and plenty of rich soil as soon as the land was cleared. More people kept coming, and my father built a sawmill and Lucius Bram started a blacksmith shop. The Bram Iron and Steel Works are still here, although they've moved outside the town. The blacksmith shop was right where the corner of Main and Willow is now.

There was quite a little settlement, and people thought it should have a name. My father wanted to call it Pleasant Grove, but Mr. Bram said there were Pleasant Groves everywhere and it ought to be named for somebody. There were all kinds of suggestions — names of people who were famous at the time — but finally Mr. Bram said the town should be named for the first baby born here. He said when babies are born in a town, it means it is a growing community. A lot of people had brought children with them, and several of the women were expecting babies about then, but there hadn't actually been any born here. I was born the next week, so the town was called Templeton. My mother wanted to name me after her father, and you can't call a town Mortimer. Lucius Bram, Junior, was born two days later, so you see it might have been Bramville."

"That would make a good opening scene for our pageant," Miss Hartley said. "Tell me some more. What about this Bram who was the first mayor?"

Mr. Temple told her about the first election and she said, "Was that really what happened? Miss Bram didn't tell us that."

"Gospel truth," Mr. Temple assured her with a smile. "I was a baby then, but my father often told the story, and so did Lucius Bram. Lucinda always was a stuffy girl. She's too concerned with her own dignity. Someday I'm going to go to one of her Historical Society meetings and liven things up."

"Did you know each other?" Miss Hartley asked.

"I didn't think she was that old. I mean . . ."

"We're getting you confused," Mrs. Temple said. "She was born after we were struck by lightning, but of course we know her. She's seen us once or twice, but she'd die sooner than admit she saw a ghost."

"I don't suppose you could manage a barn raising on your stage, could you?" Mr. Temple suggested. "They were a lot of fun. We had some exciting hunting parties, too. Serena, do you remember the time your brother brought a bear home?"

"They could have a quilting bee," Mrs. Temple said. "Or how about a threshing party? Remember the time the threshers were at Alvin Mayhew's place and Samantha had a big kettle of possum stew on the fire? It was such a big kettle she had to cook in the yard. The pig got loose somehow and ran right through the fire, knocking the kettle over. While Samantha was trying to pick it up and salvage some of the stew, the pig came round again and one of the boys picked that big kettle up and popped it right down on the pig. How that pig did squeal! I never saw Samantha so mad."

"It might be hard for them to train a pig," Mortimer said.

"There was the time we boys got mad at John Barton and put his cow in the hayloft. He never did figure out how she got up there."

"I don't suppose the time we haunted Amelia Temple away from here is very historical," Mrs. Temple said.

"It wasn't even very nice," her husband replied. "I never could see why you took such a dislike to the poor woman."

"Why wouldn't I dislike her, moving in here almost before we were properly buried and then complaining from morning till night that the house didn't suit her?"

"Then what happened?" Miss Hartley asked. She had always been curious about the ghost family.

"Another of my nephews was living with his wife and baby in the old cabin. They moved in, and they were a nice couple. They named their first daughter Serena after my wife. Many's the night Serena rocked that baby so they could sleep, and they never knew. They raised a fine family with Serena's help. If it hadn't been for her, little Johnnie would have drowned in the millpond, but he grew up and lived here too, after his father died. He was the one who put in the modern improvements. He had one of the first bathrooms in Templeton, and the first cook stove. It's still here, as you can see."

"I used to cook on the fireplace when we lived in this house," Mrs. Temple said, "but I soon learned to manage the stove. Mary Temple never did know why her gravy was better when she had company than it was when she was here alone. She lived to be an old woman and never did learn to make good gravy. I always stirred it when there was company because then she was too busy to notice."

"Their children all moved out west," Mr. Temple said. "When Mary was old and living here alone

129

she had to mortgage the house. Times were hard just then. She died before she got the mortgage paid, so the bank owns the house, but they won't get rid of us till we're ready to go."

"She can't put all that in the pageant," Mortimer said. "Tell about the time everybody thought there was a spy here. Or about building the first school."

It was quite late when Miss Hartley went home, and she had plenty of material for the pageant.

When she told Mr. Martin what she had learned, he asked, "Are you sure all this is true?"

"It must be," Miss Hartley said. "I got it from the oldest inhabitant."

"It doesn't sound like what Miss Bram told us. I thought the first settlers were dignified, hard-working people. You're going to make them sound as if they were always going hunting and having parties. Anyway, it should make a good pageant. That's the main thing."

The
Class
Picnic

IT WAS THE LAST WEEK OF SCHOOL, and everybody was restless. Miss Hartley was grading arithmetic tests and keeping one eye on the children, who were supposed to be writing compositions called, "Something Important I Have Learned in School This Year." The class did not look as if it found this topic very interesting, and Miss Hartley was beginning to wish she had assigned one called, "What I Would Rather Be Doing." But at least they were all there and not making too much noise, which was about all Miss Hartley hoped for the last week of school. Only one desk was empty, though at that one a pencil was busily writing on a sheet of ruled paper. Wilbur loved to write.

Suddenly she remembered something and said, "Oh, my goodness, I forgot to send the attendance to the office. Mr. Graham will think we're all absent. Who'd like to take it for me?"

Nearly everyone wanted to; even Wilbur appeared and waved his hand in the air. "Please could I take it, Miss Hartley?" he asked. "I've never taken anything to the office."

"All right, Wilbur. If Mrs. Clark isn't there, just put it on her desk. Someone will find it."

Wilbur took the attendance sheet, but before he was out the door he had vanished again. "Oh dear," Miss Hartley said. "You'd better go after him, William. Either make Wilbur appear or give the paper to Mrs. Clark yourself. You know how excited she gets. Hurry."

Willie hurried out the door and down the hall. Mr. Graham was coming the other way, and he was somewhat surprised to see a sheet of paper floating toward him with Willie Snodgrass running after it saying, "Wait for me." Mr. Graham caught the paper and said, "Are you taking this to the office, William? You shouldn't play with it on the way." He tried to hand the paper to Willie, but it resisted him. He pulled a little harder, and the paper started to tear.

Willie came up and put a hand on it. He said, "Thank you, Mr. Graham; it got away from me. I'll take it now."

Mr. Graham watched while the paper floated down the hall with Willie's hand on top of it. Then he shrugged and muttered, "I really do need a vacation."

As soon as he was out of sight, Willie said, "Miss Hartley says either you have to appear or I have to give the attendance to Mrs. Clark. She's getting kind of old, and we wouldn't want to give her a heart attack."

Wilbur said, "I'm sorry, I forgot," and appeared again. When the boys got to the office, they saw Mrs. Clark sitting at her desk. She was a very fat woman who wheezed. She smiled at the boys and asked, "Is that the third-grade attendance? I was just wondering where it was. Are you a new boy?"

"This is Wilbur Temple," Willie said.

"My grandmother was a Temple," Mrs. Clark said. "Maybe we're related. She was born in the Temple House on Oak Street. That was before it was haunted, of course." She laughed wheezily at her own joke and Willie said, "Wilbur's kind of new here," before Wilbur could embarrass him by say-saying he had probably played with Mrs. Clark's grandmother when she was a baby. There were times when he wished Wilbur could be more like an ordinary boy.

When the boys got back to their room, Miss Hartley said, "Mr. Graham was just here to tell us we're going on a picnic tomorrow. Alan Spencer's mother has invited our whole class to have a picnic in the Spencers' yard, and she says if it rains we can go in the barn."

Alan beamed and said, "We have a brook where you can wade, and the cat has new kittens in the barn. Be sure to wear your old clothes."

"That's right," Miss Hartley said. "Everybody bring a picnic lunch and wear old clothes. You girls may wear slacks if you want to. We'll leave right after roll call and spend the day."

The next morning everyone was so happy and excited that Miss Hartley could scarcely get them to sit still long enough for her to take attendance. When she had finished she asked, "Where's Wilbur? Isn't he coming?"

"Here I am," Wilbur said, and appeared in his school clothes.

Jimmy said, "Wilbur's not wearing play clothes."

"I wasn't thinking," Wilbur said. "Wait a minute." He vanished and reappeared, wearing faded blue jeans, a plaid shirt that looked a little too small, and dirty sneakers. "Is this better?" he asked.

"That's fine," Miss Hartley said laughing. She was wearing dark blue pedal pushers and a pink shirt.

"Please remember that my mother isn't used to ghosts," Alan said. "Don't do anything to frighten her, Wilbur."

"Have you all got your lunches?" Miss Hartley asked. "Let's go, but please walk quietly until we're out of the building."

When they got to Alan's house, they found Alan's mother and little sister waiting for them. Alan's mother said she was very happy to see them and she was glad it was such a nice day for a picnic. "You may play anywhere on our property," she

said, "but if you go in the barn, don't get too close
to the mother cat or she'll hide her kittens. Just look
at them from a distance. You can play at the other
end of the barn without disturbing her, though.
Here, Annie, you come with me."

"Can't I play with Alan?" his little sister asked.

"Not this time," her mother said. "Come along."
Annie walked backward until she fell over her sand
box. Then she sat down and started poking at the
sand.

The children raced around the yard, trying to see everything at once. Alan took them into the barn and pointed to the mother cat, who was lying on an old blanket in the corner with her kittens. "Don't go any closer than this," Alan said. "The kittens haven't even got their eyes open yet, and the mother's awful scary."

Then he took everybody to the brook and showed them how he could climb a tree and inch along one of the branches until he could drop down on the other side of the brook. He had to wade back, so everybody went wading and tried to catch minnows and polliwogs in their hands until they were all so wet that Miss Hartley said they had better go back in the sun and play baseball until they were good and dry again.

Wilbur had never played baseball until this spring, and he loved it. He stood in line, waiting for his turn at bat and humming happily to himself, but when his turn came and he picked up the bat, Alan said, "What did I tell you, Wilbur? If my mother looks out the window and sees the bat swinging itself, she'll faint." Wilbur appeared, but as usual he couldn't concentrate when he was visible and he struck out. "Maybe you'd better not play this time, Wilbur," Bobby said. "You'll just make us lose."

Then Wilbur drifted over to where the girls were jumping rope and offered to hold one end. The girls were glad to let him because they liked jumping better than holding, and they had to hold until someone missed. He stood happily in the sun, swinging his end of the rope. The girls didn't care whether they could see him or not, but Annie wandered over from her sand box and asked, "How do you make the rope stay up like that?" Wilbur immediately appeared and Annie laughed and said, "Do it again."

Her mother came out to take her in, but just then Miss Hartley called, "Lunchtime. Won't you and Annie have lunch with us, Mrs. Spencer?"

"We'd love to," Alan's mother said, "and I have a surprise for you after lunch. Come on, Annie, you bring the lunch out and I'll carry the lemonade." They went in the house and came right out again. Annie was carrying a basket and Mrs. Spencer had two big jugs of lemonade. Annie sat beside Wilbur and kept smiling at him and then ducking her head down so he couldn't see her. After lunch, Mrs. Spencer went back and got the surprise — sweet, cool Popsicles — and they all sat around licking them till there wasn't a drop left. Then Mrs. Spencer said it was Annie's nap time. Annie wanted to stay and play so badly that Mrs. Spencer finally carried her to the house, yelling so loud they could still hear her after she was inside.

Miss Hartley suggested a game of tag. That was fun until Louise whined, "It's not fair for Wilbur to tag me when I can't see him, is it, Miss Hartley? Make him stop." Miss Hartley told Wilbur that he really had to appear when he was playing tag.

Wilbur found a ball and started bouncing it until Alan said, "For goodness sake, Wilbur, either appear or go off into the woods where my mother can't see you from the house. I already asked you once. What will she think if she looks out and sees a ball bouncing by itself?"

"That's right, Wilbur," Willie said. "It's a lot more fun when we can see you. Try not to vanish so much."

"I'm sorry," Wilbur said in a tearful voice. He drifted over to Annie's sand box and let the sand run through his fingers. Miss Hartley sat down against a rock and basked in the sun, while the boys started a game of catch with the ball Wilbur had been bouncing. After a while Wilbur started building a sand castle. When Annie came out after her nap, she was enchanted to see the sand piling itself into a castle. Wilbur was feeling so miserable that he didn't even notice her until she got a stick and poked it through a leaf and put it on the top of the castle. "There, that's a flag," she said.

Wilbur immediately stopped playing with the sand and watched Annie dig a moat around her castle. Her mother came out and sat down on the edge of the sand box with Annie.

"Look, Mommy," Annie said. "The sand made itself into a castle."

"Did it, honey?" her mother replied. "I expect one of Alan's friends built it while you were in the house."

"It built itself," Annie insisted, but her mother just laughed and hugged her. Miss Hartley sat down beside Mrs. Spencer and started telling her how much the class was enjoying having all that room for the picnic.

All of a sudden Louise came running from the barn, crying and calling Miss Hartley. Everyone else came to see what the trouble was. "Calm down, Louise, and tell me what's wrong," Miss Hartley said. "Are you hurt?"

"I wanted to pet the kittens," Louise sobbed, "and I went so quietly, but the mother cat saw me and started to carry one of the kittens away. I tried to grab her, because I knew you didn't want her to hide them, and there was a place where the floor was broken and the kitten fell right through it, and

now the kitten's down at the bottom of the hole and it's crying, and the mother cat is sitting by the hole and crying too. I didn't mean to do anything."

"I told you not to get close," Alan said crossly. "You're such a dumb girl. Now we'll never get the kitten back and it's all your fault. I hate you. There isn't any way to get under that floor."

"Calm down," his mother said. "Maybe Daddy can take another piece of floor off when he gets home, and then he could climb down and get the kitten for you."

"It'll starve by that time," Alan whined. "I hate you, Louise."

"Don't say that," his mother snapped.

Miss Hartley was looking very thoughtful. "I'm sorry Louise was so naughty," she said, "but I think I know how to get the kitten back if everybody will stay out of the barn."

Willie grinned and said, "Oh yes, I bet we could get it back."

"I'm afraid there's no way to get under the barn floor, Miss Hartley," Mrs. Spencer said, "and it's too far to reach down through the hole. We keep saying we'll patch it, but then we never do."

Miss Hartley said, "Alan, I expect Wilbur's in the woods. Go get him and tell him to meet me at the barn right away."

"But what can Wilbur do?" Mrs. Spencer asked. "Even if he's very good with animals, I don't think he could persuade the mother cat to jump down and bring the kitten back. I don't think she could get back carrying a kitten."

"If anyone can do it, Wilbur can," Miss Hartley said. "He's a very unusual child. Now I'm going to the barn. The rest of you stay here, please."

"That's right," Mrs. Spencer said. "We don't want to frighten the mother cat any more. Don't cry, Louise. Sit down."

Wilbur drifted after Miss Hartley and appeared as soon as they were inside the barn. Alan ran up from the woods and said, "I can't find him anywhere, Miss Hartley. Do you think he went home? Oh, there you are, Wilbur; where were you?"

"He was by the sand box all the time," Miss Hartley said. "I just didn't want to frighten your mother."

Wilbur drifted to the corner of the barn and peered through the hole. The mother cat ruffled her fur and looked around, but she didn't move. Wilbur could see the kitten lying on the ground and hear its tiny mews. He drifted down through the floor and picked up the kitten. He handed it up through the hole, and Alan took it and cuddled it. Wilbur drifted out again and reappeared.

"Gee, thanks," Alan said. "Thanks a lot. Gosh, I didn't know how we were going to get him back, and he's my favorite. Do you want to hold him a minute?" He handed the kitten to Wilbur and yelled, "It's all right, Mom; Wilbur got the kitten back."

Wilbur laughed and said, "If you shriek in my ear like that, I'll vanish again, Alan."

"I'm sorry," Alan said. "It's just that I was so glad to get him back."

Mrs. Spencer walked over to the barn and said, "Wonderful. How did you do it? You must have a magic touch, Wilbur. Now I'll give the kitten back to its mother." When she came out of the barn, she said, "The mother has the kitten back, and they both seem to be happy. Would you like to have a kitten when they're big enough, Wilbur?"

"I'd love one," Wilbur replied, "but maybe I ought to ask my mother."

Then it was time to go, and Miss Hartley said, "Thank you very much for having us, Mrs. Spencer. This was a perfect day. It was a wonderful picnic."

"Thank you," everybody echoed her. "Thank you. Good-bye, Mrs. Spencer. Good-bye, Annie."

The
School
Play

Miss Hartley glared at Mr. Martin and said, "No, I positively will not help with the costumes the night of the pageant. I helped write the thing, I've been at every rehearsal, and I'm not going to do any more. I'm going to watch it from the audience."

Mr. Martin said gloomily that if that was how she felt, he supposed they could find a room mother to help with the costumes.

"Anyway, I have guests coming," Miss Hartley said. "The people who gave me all the information about the history of Templeton said they'd come if I'd sit with them. I think that's the least I can do after all their help. Don't you?"

"I suppose so," Mr. Martin said. "I wish I could think of a good excuse, too."

"If I'm not right there where she can see me, maybe that child who plays the nurse in the Civil War scene won't turn around and say, 'Miss Hartley, this bandage won't go on,' the way she does at every rehearsal," Miss Hartley said.

"I don't believe it," Mr. Martin said. "She's said it so often she thinks it's part of the play."

The night of the play, Miss Hartley went to the Temples' house in her new blue convertible. She was just starting to get out of the car when Mrs. Temple said, "This is very nice of you, Miss Hartley. I've never been in a car before."

Miss Hartley only jumped a little and replied, "Good evening, Mrs. Temple. I was just going in to get you. Is Mr. Temple here, too?"

"Right here," Mr. Temple said.

"I was hoping you'd decide to be visible tonight," Miss Hartley said as she started the car and drove slowly down Oak Street.

There was a gasp in her ear, and Mrs. Temple exclaimed, "I didn't know you'd go so fast! Is it safe?"

"I'm only doing twenty," Miss Hartley told her. "You can't drive fast on these streets."

"Mercy, I hope we won't go on a street where you can go fast, then," Mrs. Temple said. "Feel the wind. My goodness."

"Won't you appear for me?" Miss Hartley asked. "I'll feel silly sitting beside two empty seats."

"I've been practicing modern clothes," Mr. Tem-

144

ple told her. "I'll appear when we get out of the car, and you can tell me how I look. I'm not really used to these high speeds either."

Since Mrs. Temple was determined not to appear in the auditorium, she sat between her husband and Miss Hartley. Miss Hartley didn't want anyone to try to sit in the seat that looked empty. "You'll have to learn to appear in modern clothes before the end of the month," Mr. Temple said. "This would be a good time to practice."

Miss Hartley wanted to know what was going to happen at the end of the month. "Why, it's very exciting," Mrs. Temple said. "Really, it's almost like a story book. Do you remember those pictures that your brother and his friend took — the ones that were in a magazine?" Miss Hartley nodded. "You'll hardly believe it, but my husband's brother's grandson saw them and he recognized the house at once. He is getting old, and apparently he's terribly rich. He telephoned the mayor all the way from New Mexico to say he wanted to buy the house and give it to the village for a museum. Isn't it amazing? Mr. Montrose came today to tell us about it. He says we can stay in the house as long as we want to if we'll just show people around. I think it will be fun."

"There's only one trouble," Mr. Temple said. "This Alden Temple is coming here at the end of the month to sign the papers, and Mr. Montrose wants to introduce us and tell him we're willing to act as caretakers. Mr. Montrose is afraid he wouldn't like the idea of ghosts living in his museum, so Serena has to learn to appear in modern clothes before he comes. I think I'm doing it very well, don't you?"

"You look wonderful," Miss Hartley assured him. "Listen, Mrs. Temple. I could come to your house and you could practice on me. Maybe that would help you get used to it. Oh, here comes Miss Bram to make her speech. Why does she have to? This was supposed to be a school play."

"For the last fifty years or so, Miss Bram hasn't allowed anything of historical interest to happen in Templeton without making a speech," Mr. Temple explained. "She took up history when Bradford Wells jilted her. Remind me to tell you about that sometime. He had a narrow escape."

"Sh," Mrs. Temple said. "She's beginning."

Miss Bram still looked very imposing, and her voice easily filled the auditorium. She told the audience, which was largely composed of the actors' families, that people didn't pay enough attention to history and that the school was doing them a great service by reminding them of some of the important events in Templeton's history. She went on at some length, but at last she said, "The mayor told me today that Templeton is going to have its own historical museum in the old Temple place. I shall look forward to seeing all of you there." Then she sat down.

"Is she going to run our museum?" Mrs. Temple gasped, but Mr. Temple told her not to worry.

At last the pageant began.

The first scene went very well. The settlers walked to the middle of the stage and said, "We will build our houses by this river." Then the curtains were pulled back a little farther to reveal a few log cabins beside the river, which was a long strip of blue paper. Mortimer and some other boys paced back and forth beside the river, wondering when the babies would be born. Then Janie Snodgrass walked on, carrying a large doll, and said, "This is my new brother. His name is Mortimer Temple," and everybody cheered. They clapped and laughed when Barbara Snodgrass, who was sitting with her parents, said, "Look at Janie with my doll."

When the curtains opened for the next scene, there were log cabins on both sides of the river. Two boys were addressing a crowd of people. One of them said, "You all know me. I've been a good blacksmith, and I'll be a good mayor. If I'm elected, I'll build new roads and a new bridge. A vote for Lucius Bram is a vote for good government."

The other boy said, "A vote for John Barton is a vote for progress. I will build a new school and a better bridge. Remember, go to the mill tomorrow and vote for John Barton." The two orators debated a while longer and then went home. Mortimer suddenly appeared in the middle of the stage and said, "Everybody who lives on the south side of the river wants Lucius Bram for mayor because he lives on the south side and his blacksmith shop is there, too. The people who live north of the river want John Barton because his farm is north of the river. What will happen tomorrow?" Then he vanished, and the audience gasped.

Mrs. Temple whispered, "I told that boy not to show off," but Mr. Temple just laughed.

The lights were lowered, and a voice from the stage said, "Now it is night. Tomorrow is the day of our first election." A figure could be seen creeping across the stage in the dark. It looked like the boy who had been telling people to vote for Lucius Bram. He was carrying a saw, and when he got to the bridge, he sawed off the posts that held it up. The bridge, which was just a plank, collapsed onto the blue paper to the sound of a loud splash offstage. The boy picked up the plank and his saw and crept away. The curtain closed and there was a lot of noise from the stage.

When the curtains were opened again and the lights came on, the audience could see several rowboats pulled up on the south bank of the river. The voice from the stage said, "Now it is Election Day. The men have done their chores and they are going to vote." When the men on the north side of the river saw the bridge gone and all the boats on the wrong side of the river, they jumped up and down and yelled. One of them said, "We'll swim across." But the others said the river was too swift after all the rain. John Barton said, "We'll go to the next bridge. It's only six miles. We may be in time." The men ran off the stage. When they came back in sight, they were panting and running along the other side of the river, but just as they got to the mill, a man came out and locked the door. "Polls are closed," he announced. "Lucius Bram's our new mayor by a unanimous vote."

John Barton said, "I will throw him in the river," and the curtains closed to the sound of another loud splash and a lot of yelling and laughter.

Miss Bram jumped up and said, "That's not what

happened. My grandfather . . ." but before she could say any more Mr. Graham went up and spoke to her. Nobody could hear what he said, but Miss Bram sat down again.

After that there were scenes showing the first school, the nurse in the Civil War hospital, the railroad coming to Templeton, the first airplane ride by a local citizen, and finally a big parade with almost the whole school in it, for the end of the Second World War. The band led the parade, and Miss Hartley saw that Mr. Angell had found another glockenspiel for Mortimer. Miss Hartley wanted to ask how he had explained himself to Mr. Angell, but there was so much noise that Mrs. Temple couldn't hear her.

When everyone was leaving, Miss Hartley took the Temples to find Wilbur and Mortimer so they could go home. Mr. Temple had been visible all evening, but when a woman with two little boys bumped into him, he vanished. They found the room where the boys were changing. Mortimer was appearing alternately in his costume and his band uniform, but everybody was too busy to pay any attention to him.

Miss Bram burst in, followed by Mr. Graham and Mr. Martin, and said, "Is that the young woman who is responsible for the slander about my grandfather?"

Mr. Temple appeared for a moment in his old-fashioned clothes and said, "Lucinda, you know every word of that was true. Your grandfather made a good mayor, and the first thing he did was build a good strong bridge, just as he promised when he was campaigning. My father helped him build it. He helped him row all the boats across that night, too. Lucius Bram was a fine man, but he never left anything to chance."

Miss Bram said, "Perhaps you're right." She seemed very subdued.

Mr. Temple said, "It's all a long time ago now. Come on, boys, let's go home." They drifted out and left Mr. Graham and Mr. Martin staring.

Summer
Ahead

Miss Hartley was taking attendance on the last day of school. When she came to Wilbur, he answered, but he appeared so faintly that Miss Hartley exclaimed, "Wilbur! I can see right through you! Don't you feel well?"

"I'm sorry," Wilbur said. He became more visible, but Miss Hartley saw that he was wearing the dingy-looking gray shirt he always appeared in when he was worried or unhappy. She didn't understand it, but she thought maybe he couldn't think bright colors if he didn't feel cheerful.

"I hope everybody's feeling strong today because we have a lot to do," Miss Hartley said after roll call. "We must put everything away for next year, and clean our desks too."

The big window sill was already empty except

for a small cactus that Miss Hartley was going to take home for the summer, and Miss Hartley had cleaned her own desk that morning before anyone else was there, so there was nothing on it but a pile of report cards and a pencil. The children kept looking at the report cards until Miss Hartley said, "I'm not going to hand them out till it's time to go home, but I'll tell you this much. You all passed and . . ."

Marilyn raised her hand, and Miss Hartley said, "Yes, Marilyn?"

"May Kathy and I put the puzzles in the boxes and put them away, Miss Hartley?"

"That will be fine, and Alan and Jason had better put all the books on the top shelf of the cupboard, because they're both tall. Wilbur, could you hold this chair steady while I stand on it and take the alphabet strip down? William, you catch it so it doesn't tear, and roll it around this tube."

"I bet Wilbur could float up and take the pieces of tape off for you," Willie suggested. "Remember how you and Mortimer decorated the Christmas tree, Wilbur?"

"Could you really do that, Wilbur?" Miss Hartley asked.

"Sure," Wilbur said. "Watch." He vanished and in a minute the first piece of tape came off. Everyone watched as the end of the long strip of paper came lower and lower. As soon as Willie could reach it, he started rolling it around the tube.

Just then the door opened and Mr. Graham came

in. "Good morning, Miss Hartley," he said. "Oh dear, you shouldn't let William pull the paper down that way. He'll tear it. Stand on a chair and unfasten the tape carefully. Then you'll be able to use that alphabet again next year." While he was talking, Wilbur continued to take the pieces of tape off the wall until he had the whole alphabet strip free. Mr. Graham watched the end float gently down and stay still while Willie rolled it up. He shook his head and said, "Well, it worked all right this time, but I still think my way is better. I just came in to wish everyone a good vacation and tell you not to spend the whole summer studying. I'll see you next year."

Everybody laughed and said, "Good-bye, Mr. Graham. See you in the fall."

"Now we'd better clear our desks," Miss Hartley said. "Bobby, when the wastebasket gets full, would

you empty it in the boiler room? What's everybody going to do this summer?"

"Kathy and I are going to day camp," Nina said.

"Are you? I am, too!" Margery exclaimed. "It'll be fun. We get to go swimming."

"We're going to visit my grandparents in Canada," Bobby said. "We go there every summer."

Several of the children said they were going to visit their gandparents when Louise shouted, "Look, Miss Hartley. Here's my jump rope that I lost."

"I told you I didn't take it," Bobby said. "Did all that stuff come out of your desk? No wonder you lose everything."

"Louise, you sure better learn to raise your hand before next year," Alan said. "You know what Mrs. Westen will do to you if you ever talk out like that. Gosh, my brother had her a couple of years ago and she used to put him in the hall if he even sneezed."

"You didn't raise yours, either," Louise said.

"I wasn't speaking to Miss Hartley," Alan explained.

Louise raised her hand and made a face at Alan. "Yes, Louise?" Miss Hartley said.

"What'll Mrs. Westen do to Wilbur? I bet she won't allow a ghost in her room for a minute. I bet he won't even be able to come back to school unless he fails."

"If Wilbur can't be in the fourth grade, then I won't either," Willie said. "I'll just stay in the third grade the rest of my life."

"You mustn't talk that way," Miss Hartley said. "Mrs. Westen has been here a long time, and she's an excellent teacher. I'm sure you could all learn a lot from her, but . . ."

"My mother had Mrs. Westen," Nina said. "She says she bets next year she won't hear any more about ghosts, because Mrs. Westen would never allow such silliness in her class."

"Miss Hartley, couldn't we stay in your class next year?" Kathy asked. "I'll never be able to do my arithmetic without Wilbur, and I bet Willie won't either. He's even worse than I am."

"Maybe you could go to Wilbur's house after school every day and get him to show you," Jason suggested. "Where is he, anyway?"

"I'm right here," Wilbur said.

"Well for goodness sake, you ought to appear for the last day. We might not see you again till next year. Don't you even want to say good-bye to us?"

Wilbur appeared, but he looked very gloomy. The gray shirt looked even dingier.

"What's the matter, Wilbur?" Miss Hartley asked. "Don't you feel well?"

Wilbur sniffed and said, "I'm all right." Then he said, "I wish we could have school all summer."

Everybody groaned. "You're crazy," Bobby said. "Summer's the only time we can have any fun. I can hardly wait."

"I can't wait till July," Louise said. "My sister's going to Girl Scout camp, and I get to have our room all to myself for two whole weeks. I'm going to sleep in the top bunk every night and have company if I want to, and I won't have to be quiet so she can listen to her old radio."

"Well, I can't wait till swimming lessons start," Willie said. "Alan and Jason and I are going together. Hey, Wilbur, why don't you come too? I bet we could scare the swimming teacher half to death. Wouldn't that be neat?"

"Do you think I could?" Wilbur asked hopefully.

"I don't know," Alan said. "We might all get put out if Wilbur did anything."

Wilbur sniffed again and Miss Hartley asked, "Do you have any plans for the summer, Wilbur?"

"Mr. Montrose is going to send a lot of men to fix our house up so it can be a museum," Wilbur said. "They're going to put in a telephone and new wiring and a lot of stuff. He made us promise not to do a single thing to scare them. And I never get

157

to go play at anybody else's house because they're always afraid I'll scare their mothers or something. I won't have anything to do all summer, and maybe Mrs. Westen won't even let me come to school in the fall."

"I was trying to tell you . . ." Miss Hartley began when Jason waved his hand so violently that she stopped and said, "What's the matter, Jason?"

"I've got a great idea," Jason exclaimed. "You know that big field behind our house? Well maybe you don't know, but there is one. It belongs to the man in the next block, and there's a brook running through it and trees all around."

"You mean Mr. Fistler's field," Alan said. "He used to have a big vegetable garden there. It's the same brook that runs through our lot."

"Quit interrupting. Who cares if it's the same brook? If you'd let me talk for a minute, I'd tell you my idea. Mr. Fistler told my father that if we'd keep the field mowed, we kids could play there whenever we wanted to. We can climb the trees and pick the apples, or build a tree house or anything. We might even be able to camp out overnight sometimes. You can't even see the field from the the house because of the trees. Wilbur could play there with us any time. Gosh, Wilbur, if you get a telephone, it'll be neat, because then we can call each other up and you'll know when to meet us and what we're going to do and everything."

"I know Mr. Fistler," Willie said. "My father cuts his hair. That would be perfect. Better than day camp, because we can play ball or do anything we want to and not have to look at a lot of bugs and leaves and say what kind they are. Oh, Wilbur, won't it be fun? And I bet you can take swimming if you want to. Ask your father. And if Mrs. Westen won't let you come to school next year, I'll stop at your house every day and tell you what we did."

"I've been trying all morning to tell you . . ." Miss Hartley began, but the door opened.

"Miss Morrison," the class shouted. "Hi, Miss Morrison. Are you on vacation?"

"Better than that," Miss Morrison said with a smile. "My, I'm glad to see you. Did everybody pass, Miss Hartley? Have you told them?"

"I've been trying all morning, but they never give me a chance to talk. What do you suppose Mrs. Westen would do with a class like this?"

"Make them stay in the hall forever, I should think," Miss Morrison said. "I remember when I had her I was scared every minute. May I tell them, Miss Hartley?"

Miss Hartley smiled and nodded, and Miss Morrison said, "I graduated last week, and I'm going to teach school next year. I asked Mr. Graham if he needed a teacher here, and he said Mr. Westen has retired from his job and wants to move away, so of course Mrs. Westen is going with him, and I'm going to teach the fourth grade right here."

Everybody laughed and clapped.

Louise raised her hand.

"My goodness," Miss Morrison said. "Yes, Louise?"

"Will you let Wilbur come to school?"

"I certainly will. It wouldn't be the same class without him. Where is Wilbur?"

Wilbur appeared at his desk, smiling broadly. Then he vanished again, and when he reappeared he was wearing a new green and white plaid shirt. Miss Morrison said, "I'm glad to see you, Wilbur. You look fine. Do you suppose I could meet your family this summer?"

Then the bell rang and Miss Hartley said, "Time to go home. Line up and I'll give you your report cards. I hope everybody has a wonderful summer."

"I think summer will be just as good as school," Wilbur said happily.